Wheeling and Dealing

The Sisters, Texas Mystery Series

Book 18

BECKI WILLIS

Editing by SJS Editorial Services
Cover by Diana Buidoso dienel96 & Anelia Savova

ISBN: 978-1-947686-26-7

CONTENTS

1

It was the least desirable location in the restaurant, situated between a busy kitchen and the musty-smelling storeroom. The swing of either door was a hazard to anyone occupying the table. The spot was noisy, hot, and had poor lighting. Even the staff avoided it during breaktime.

Yet a lone diner sat peacefully eating his dinner in the dreaded spot, content with the awkwardly placed table.

Another man intruded on his meal. Uninvited, the man took a seat and demanded, "What are you doing here?" The growled words were low, despite the clamor coming from the kitchen.

The first man motioned to his half-empty plate. "What does it look like I'm doing? I'm eating."

"We agreed you wouldn't come here."

"Change of plans." The diner's manner remained placid.

"You didn't tell me about a change."

"I'm telling you now." The man placed his fork on his plate and looked his companion in the eye. His voice tightened. "I decided to come. I like the food."

"I can see that."

Picking his fork back up, the diner resumed his meal. "Relax. I won't be here long. Just long enough for a good meal and a quick look around."

"I don't want you here yet. Things are still in the early stages. It takes time to get an operation like this up and running."

"I know that, Pops. I'm just trying to get a feel for the place."

"That can wait. You'll be back soon enough, and you can get your feel then."

"No one will remember seeing me in here. Why do you think I chose the crappiest seat in the house?"

"To bum a free meal off the owner?" the older man suggested.

His companion laughed. "That's a good one. But, seriously, how are we on recruits?"

"I'm working on getting a few more. Some of the ones I have are new. It's too early to know how they'll work out."

"Nothing wrong with being new," the diner said. Finished with his meal, he pushed away the empty plate. "When we first started this, we were new, too. We didn't do too bad, now did we?"

"We made a few mistakes along the way, but I think it all evened out in the end."

"End? What end?"

"There's always an end."

"Don't be a pessimist."

"Don't be careless," the second man countered. "You coming here could compromise everything."

"You need to relax. Everything is going according to plan." His partner sounded calm and confident. "We'll do this the way we always have. You handle the wheels. I'll handle the deals."

2

"I swear, I leave town for two weeks, and the whole town goes to the devil in a tow sack!" Bertha Cessna grumbled.

Her granddaughter hid her amusement behind her coffee cup. "Is it really that bad?" Madison deCordova asked. She was accustomed to Granny Bert's outbursts. The octogenarian was never shy about voicing her opinion.

A look of annoyance pushed a wave of wrinkles across the older woman's face. She didn't appreciate being doubted. "I suppose you haven't kept up with the latest news circling around town."

"Not really," Madison admitted. "Between the hospital and then rehab, we're still getting acclimated to being home."

"I know it's been hard on you," her grandmother relented. "You and Brash have been through the wringer these last few weeks."

Madison's expelled breath spoke volumes. "It's been quite an ordeal," she agreed.

Not long ago, someone had staged a series of attacks against area first responders. No branch of service was safe. Nurses, deputies, medics, and a clinic attendant had all been injured. Most tragically, a volunteer fireman had lost his life during the all-out assaults.

As the chief of police in The Sisters, her husband had been in the direct line of fire. While trying to shield his deputy from greater harm, Brash took the brunt of the attack. His brush with death made Madison realize the full weight of the badge he and so many others carried. He was finally home after weeks of supervised care, but they all knew he faced an uphill journey toward full recovery.

"You still haven't told me how the town has gone to the devil. And in a tow sack, no less," Madison said.

"That smile of yours won't last long when you hear the news. We have real trouble brewing here in The Sisters."

"What kind of trouble?"

"The kind you get when you mix an incompetent acting chief of police with drug dealers." Granny Bert slapped the table hard enough to jostle their cups. "Otis Perry has no business being in charge!" She all but spat the man's name.

Unfortunately for the town, Senior Deputy Otis Perry was temporarily filling Brash's position. Brash insisted the older man had good instincts and was a capable lawman. The problem, however, wasn't with Perry's abilities. The problem was with his inflated ego and his determination to put his own stamp on current policy.

At the mention of drugs, the smile did, indeed, vanish from Madison's face. "What are you talking about?" Her heart ticked up a beat in panic. "Why am I just now hearing about it?"

"You had enough on your plate without this. It was also the best way to keep Brash from learning the truth. You know that man of yours. He'd insist you take him down to the station, and he'd refuse to go in a wheelchair. He'd undo all his progress and do nothing but fret over this whole situation."

"That's true," Madison admitted. "But I normally sit in on Vina's weekly updates, and she never mentioned any of this."

"Because she also knows how Brash would react. I suspect she chose to keep mum about this the same way I have. The same way his parents and Megan have."

"Megan knows?" She couldn't imagine her stepdaughter keeping something like this from them.

"She's dating a deputy. Of course she knows. And she knows how her father would react."

"Let me get this straight. Everyone kept this a secret, even from me." She tried keeping the hurt from her voice as she focused on the biggest issue. "But you're telling me now. What's changed?"

"For one thing, you're home and more likely to hear the news around town. I wanted you to hear it from one of us so you weren't blindsided."

She murmured a thank you. At least their family felt some remorse for keeping such news from them. "And for another?"

"The problems keep growing. There's been chatter about drug deals going down. A kid was expelled from school for bringing drugs on campus. A couple of small busts have been made. I think this goes deeper than a bunch of kids looking for a thrill though. Mark my words," Granny Bert predicted. "This is just the tip of the iceberg. Drugs are being delivered and distributed here in The Sisters, and Otis Perry is too full of himself to see it."

Madison looked thoughtful. "You think the motorcycle gang is back? I know they were trying to sell more than just marijuana before. And they certainly stirred up enough trouble around town." She thought of the way the men had harassed Megan, and the way they left locals feeling vulnerable. No merchant could summon the courage to stand up to them over alleged thefts. Madison's voice took on a mournful note when she admitted, "But as much as we wanted to pin the first responder attacks on them, it turned out they were innocent."

"Of that crime, anyway," her grandmother said. "Doesn't mean they're innocent of others."

"True. But I had hoped they'd moved on."

"Otis brags about how he gave them a stern warning and ran them out of town, but we know he's about as scary as a dog with no teeth. All bark, no bite. Folks are in more danger from all the hot air escaping his mouth than they are from any real action."

"You think the gang is back and pushing drugs?"

"Maybe." Granny Bert looked doubtful.

Misunderstanding her meaning, Madison's tone turned sympathetic. "Don't beat yourself up for being behind on the local news, Granny. You deserved that vacation."

Her grandmother took offense. She may have taken a two-week trip in her RV, but the octogenarian always had her finger on the pulse of the community. "Who said I was behind? My sources checked in with me every day."

Madison smiled. *Granny Bert and her sources!*

"I'm sure they did," she acknowledged. "That's why you're the undisputed head of the information network in The Sisters."

"Laugh all you want, but it's a public service to my community, and a duty I don't take lightly." She emphasized her statement with a smart nod.

"Don't get huffy on me. I meant no offense."

"None taken, but don't be thinking I was lax about

knowing what was going on." Her grandmother wagged a finger in her direction. "You know what they say."

"*If Bertha Cessna don't know it, it ain't worth knowing,*" Madison dutifully quoted the local saying.

"You're darn tootin'," she said with a smart nod. "All I'm saying is, I think it's too soon to make rash judgments about who's behind all this drug business."

"Granny, I know you pride yourself on knowing everything that happens in our community. But I think you need to tread lightly on this one. Poking your nose into something like this could be really dangerous."

"Don't you worry. My nose will be just fine."

Madison eyed her grandmother suspiciously. "Exactly what are you and your nose planning to do?"

Madison wasn't fooled by Granny Bert's casual shrug or by her innocent tone. "Oh, you know. Just ask a few questions. Gather a few facts here and there. What I always do."

"But Otis is the acting chief right now, and you know what that could mean."

"Otis is the least of my concerns. He's too busy playing boss to even notice what's going on right under his nose. He's turning a blind eye to this drug business, and it's going to be the ruin of this town!"

Madison nibbled her bottom lip. "What an inopportune time for Brash to be out on sick leave."

"Or what a perfect opportunity," Granny Bert countered.

With a tiny gasp, Madison said, "You think the timing is on purpose?"

"It makes sense. Brash is the sharpest, most capable officer this community has ever seen. Now, he's laid up in bed, and Otis is in charge. The fool is like a little banty rooster, all puffed up and cocksure, but no match for the big birds. What better time to get a foothold in

The Sisters than while Otis is in charge? We might as well hang a shingle on the city limits sign that says, 'Criminals welcome. Incompetent moron temporarily in charge.'"

It took a moment for Madison to digest what her grandmother had said. She was absolutely right. Now was the perfect time for ne'er do wells to take advantage of Brash's absence.

"Should I tell him?" she wondered aloud. "His doctors were adamant about him going back to work too soon, but this is serious stuff. I feel like he should at least know."

"He'll hit the roof when he finds out everyone kept this from him," Granny Bert agreed, "but it's for his own good. He needs to concentrate on getting the full use of his leg back. And speaking of that... When's that physical therapist coming?"

"Monday morning. Brash has the week off, so to speak, before the next round of therapy." With a sigh, she added, "The doctors warned this round could be grueling."

"If anyone's up to it, it's that man of yours. He needs to concentrate on that, not on what's happening in town."

"You're right, of course, but it still doesn't feel right keeping something like this from him."

"Let's see just how serious this is before telling him."

"*Let's*?"

"Okay, let me," she corrected. "You know most people ignore old ladies. That's what makes me so effective at doing what I do."

Madison begged to differ. "I don't think anyone can ignore you, Granny."

"I can be discreet when I want to be," her grandmother insisted. "Let me and the girls do a little investigating. If we think it's something Brash should know about, we'll cross that bridge when we get there."

"You and the *girls*" —all of whom were over eighty— "have a way of stirring up trouble, and you know it."

"And you're always right there among us, young lady," Granny Bert reminded her. "Just leave it to us. We'll poke around and find out what Otis Perry can't."

"I have a better suggestion. Why don't we let the other deputies find out what's going on? Otis isn't the only one on the force, you know."

"But he's the boss now, and he won't let the others do their jobs. He should have the deputies fighting crime, not working on his pet projects. Did you know he gave Arlene Kopetsky a ticket for going too slow? Slow, mind you, not for speeding! The man is completely incompetent!" She smacked the table again for emphasis.

The vibration rattled more than just the dishes. Paired with her grandmother's news, it rattled Madison's nerves.

Trouble was brewing, and that tow sack Granny mentioned seemed inevitable.

3

Brash took the breakfast tray from his wife with a smile. "Thanks, sweetheart."

Madison eyed the handsome man propped up against the bedstead. After a bout of grumpiness over being in 'confinement,' his brown eyes had their sparkle back, and his smile was as charming as ever.

"Ah, that's more like the husband I know and love," she said with a smile of her own.

"I know I still have my moments, but I'm doing my best to behave like a decent human being, and not a cave man."

"I know it's frustrating, but we just want you to heal."

"I am healing."

"We want you to heal properly," Madison amended. She poured coffee into his waiting cup.

Most of their meals were eaten this way now—together, yet separately. Brash's meal was served on a bed tray, his injured leg stretched out in front of him. Madison would pull a chair and folding tray close to the bedside, and they talked while eating. Other than the room and the bed, it was almost like eating in the breakfast nook.

Almost.

Digging into her own eggs, she asked in an upbeat tone, "What's on your agenda today?"

"Oh, I thought I'd start off by lying in bed. Then, I'll lie here some more. After a few hours of thinking up something interesting to do, I'll take a little nap or just lie here and rest. You know," he said, shrugging his wide shoulders, "the usual."

"I know it's boring, sweetheart, and I'm sorry."

A grumble slipped back into his words. "My back hurts from lying on it all day. I'm ready to be up and about."

"I know. But you weren't shot in the back with a poisoned arrow. You were shot in the thigh, which is why you're supposed to stay off your leg."

"I was shot in the side, too. Nicked a rib. And you know the old song. The rib bone's connected to the backbone. The backbone's connected to the hip bone..."

"Yep, and that hip bone is connected to the thighbone, where most of the damage is." She sipped on her coffee. "Too bad you don't enjoy watching television."

"A little bit goes a long way. And I've read until my eyes have crossed. That doesn't leave a lot of options."

"Visiting?"

"I appreciate the visitors. I really do. But there's only so many times we can talk about the weather, or cow prices, or what our kids are up to these days. I feel like no one's really opening up to me. Even Vina is stonewalling me. She's good to come visit, but I know she's not giving me the full picture about what's going on down at the station."

"Because you're on sick leave, Brash. That means letting someone else deal with the things down at the station for a while."

His mood darkened again as he reminded her, "You

do realize that means Otis is the one dealing with things. It's a bit like leaving Barney Fife in charge. He gets ahead of himself and forgets to do the job he was hired to do."

Madison grinned broadly. "Good analogy, except for the physical requirements. Otis is the exact opposite of Barney."

"Come to think of it, he looks more like Otis Campbell, doesn't he?"

"The old drunk that let himself in and out of the jail cell?" she asked, thinking of the old *Andy Griffith Show*. Reruns gave the old favorite perpetual life.

"That's the one."

Madison burst out laughing. "He does! That's exactly who Otis Perry looks like!" Her animated exclamation almost upended her tray. "Why did I never see that before?"

"Because Perry was never acting in my place?" he suggested.

Crinkling her nose, Madison said, "*Acting* is right. No matter who I talk to, everyone is complaining that Perry is nowhere near the caliber of chief that you are."

"He wouldn't have been my first choice as acting chief, but that was the mayor's decision, not mine."

"The next time the mayor comes to visit, you should remind him of that."

"He should be bringing me a report at the end of the week. I'll look through it and see what Perry's done in my absence."

"You mean other than issue tickets all over town? Driving too fast, driving too slow, littering, parking on the street, driving a tractor or ATV on a residential street... From what I hear, he's been on a roll."

"Technically, that last one is legit. As a rule, though, we only issue citations if they're driving irresponsibly." His forehead puckered as he added, "But there's no ordinance in either town to say cars can't park along sidewalks."

After Granny Bert's dire warning of a tow sack, Madison did her homework. Her mother-in-law, Lydia deCordova, held a close second when it came to knowing everything that happened in town. She had also spoken with Vina and Megan to get a broader view of the situation.

"Just the same, he has Nate leaving notes on the vehicles, requesting that they move."

His trademark quirked brow appeared. "Good luck with that. Unless they're causing a clear hazard or blocking their neighbor's driveway, there's nothing the law can do. There's no consequence if they choose not to comply."

"Tell your friend from Mayberry that," Madison mumbled.

"I noticed the way you skirted around my suspicion that something more is happening in town than people are telling me about. What is it, Maddy? What are y'all not saying?"

She nibbled her lower lip. The expression had almost become her own trademark. She hated keeping secrets from her husband, but Granny Bert was right. He would insist on going to the station himself and could potentially undo all his progress so far.

Avoiding a direct lie, she said, "I think you said it best yourself. Perry isn't anyone's first choice to be the acting chief."

"You're keeping something from me, Maddy. Is there something I should be aware of?"

"We just got home, sweetheart. I've been to the grocery store one time. I think someone at the department can answer that better than I can."

"Passing the buck, are you?" Brash asked with his shrewd brown gaze.

"No comment."

Determined to be a better patient than he had been previously, Brash changed the subject. "Tell me what's going on with *In a Pinch*. Is Derron holding the fort down for you?"

"You know Derron. As long as he doesn't get distracted by a big sale or some shiny bauble, he's very good at his job. He's not only managed the office and filled in at *Posey's Petals and Plants*, but he's taken on two fix-it jobs. He already put in a wheelchair ramp for one client and is now working on building some shelves for another."

"I've gotta admit. Stylish clothes and all, the man knows how to use tools. Any other jobs coming up?"

"Why?" Madison teased. "Are you applying for a part-time position?"

"Unless it can be done by phone or computer, I'm afraid I'm out."

"It's just as well. Things are a little slow right now."

He could read between the lines. "Anything to be concerned about?"

"Not really. We're normally a little busier than this, but most people know about your injuries and are being respectful of that."

"Madison, look at me." From the somber note in his voice and the use of her full name, she knew he had something serious to say. She raised her eyes to his. "I don't want you putting your career on hold while I'm recovering. You've worked too hard to build your business to back off now. *In a Pinch* is important to you, so it's important to me. You don't have to babysit me."

She gave him her 'mom' look. "Are you sure about that? I've found you out of bed more than once, you know."

"Until you started hiding my crutches," he

complained. "But this isn't about me. This is about you, and being able to spend the time you need on your business."

"I am, and I do." She reached out to take his hand. "When I started *In a Pinch*, it was as a young widow trying to provide for her teenage twins. I started the business because of my family. And if needed, I'm going to pause the business for my family. Nothing is more important than that."

"I'm out of danger, sweetheart. I may be in pain, but other than the occasional pity party that plays havoc with my mood, I'm stable. I can spend a few hours of the day by myself. And I'll be starting in-home physical therapy soon, so if there's something you need to do, I want you to do it."

She squeezed his strong hand. "I need to be here for my husband."

"And I appreciate that. Just promise me that, if someone approaches you with a job, you'll at least consider it."

"Even if it's one of those jobs where someone gets me confused with a private detective?"

"Those do make me apprehensive," he admitted. "You don't have the best track record when it comes to staying out of trouble. And this time, I won't be around to have your back."

"You always have my back, sweetheart. It may be in a different capacity this time, but I know I can always depend on you. But if it makes you feel any better, I also have Nate looking out for me now."

"That's true, and it does make me feel better." He gave her one of his heart-melting smiles. "You know what would also make me feel better?"

"What's that?"

"If I could get out of this house." Seeing the protest forming on her lips, he was quick to say, "Only to the porch. I just need a little fresh air and sunshine for a while. I've been cooped up way too long."

"You'll stay in your wheelchair?"

"I promise."

It was impossible to resist Brash's smile or his beseeching brown eyes. When he looked at her like that, she would agree to most anything.

"You, my dear husband, have yourself a deal."

Texas weather didn't take its cues from an almanac. According to the calendar, it was autumn. Retailers had already started the push for pumpkin-flavored everything. Many stores were already teasing their Christmas line, vying for space among jack-o-lanterns and witches. People from northern states posted about crisp morning air and the magnificent colors of fall.

Like most of the South, the weather here was still stuck in summer. Daytime temperatures flirted with the ninety-degree mark. The sweltering sun and the warm breath of humidity were deadlocked, each determined to outlast the other. Both would likely be around to greet November.

With the worst of the day behind them, Madison maneuvered her patient onto the front porch. By the time she got Brash up and out of the bed, into the wheelchair, and traveled from the rear of the Big House to the front, they were both exhausted.

"Whew. That was a workout," she said. "How are you? Did it hurt too badly?"

"It wasn't a picnic," he admitted. Tell-tale white lines feathered out from his mouth. His face was pinched with pain. "But the pain will pass."

She situated his leg into a comfortable position and fussed over his pillows.

"Maddy!" he finally said, his voice coming out gruffer than intended. "Just leave it be. I'm fine. Give us both time to catch our breath."

"I'll grab us some tea. Do you want the ceiling fan on before I go?"

"Actually, the heat feels good."

"Okay. I'll be back in a jiffy."

The kitchen was also at the back of the old house, so it took longer than the jiffy she predicted. She grabbed a pitcher of iced tea, added a bag of chips, some picante sauce, and a few cookies, and piled them onto a tray. After another trek across the sprawling house, she was more than ready for the porch swing.

"Think I got lost?" She smiled, settling the tray onto a small table.

"Not really. I knew you'd bring more than tea."

"Just something to tide us over until supper."

"So far, five cars have stopped in the middle of the street. Everyone wants to say hello or ask how I'm doing."

"The joys of living in a small town."

Brash accepted the tea glass and the plate of chips and dip she handed him. There was a collapsible cup holder on his chair to hold his drink. A clip-on tray had been a cheer-you-up gift from Megan.

With a rueful expression on his face, he told her, "Four of the five wanted to know when I'll be back on the job."

"At least you know they miss you."

He cocked his brown. "More like 'at least I know something is wrong down at the station.'"

Madison was running out of ways to avoid his questions about troubles in town. He would just worry if he knew the truth, and he would insist on going back to the office. Not only was it too soon, but it simply wasn't feasible. If getting him onto the porch was this exhausting, Madison couldn't imagine getting him into a vehicle.

She used one more diversionary tactic. "Here," she said, thrusting the cookie plate toward him. "These are the last of the ones Bethani made. We can tell her how much we enjoyed them, and that we're ready for a refill."

With an innocent smile, she quickly stuffed one into her own mouth.

Even if she wanted to, she couldn't answer any more questions with her mouth full.

4

Nate Stone left the station with a scowl upon his face. He admitted that he was still a newbie in his chosen career. After graduating from the police academy at the top of his class, he had come straight to work for The Sisters Police Department. Yet, it didn't take years of experience under his belt to know that Acting Chief Otis Perry wasn't handling the job with the same attention to detail as the competent but injured Chief deCordova.

They had just come from a briefing, at which time the other three deputies on the force, himself included, had expressed worry over the increased presence of drugs in their small community. The acting chief, however, barely listened to their concerns. He had his own agenda when it came to law enforcement. He was more concerned about increasing revenue for the twin cities of Naomi and Juliet—most often referred to as The Sisters—than he was about hearing his fellow deputies' input. He insisted that making more traffic stops was the best way to boost tax dollars for the community and therefore provide better safety for their citizens.

When pressed over the issue of drugs, he reasoned

that if illegal substances were being brought into the area, making more traffic stops would be 'killing two birds with one stone.'

From what Nate understood, Perry had been on the department for more years than anyone cared to remember. When hometown hero-turned-football legend-turned-policeman Brash deCordova was hired as chief of police, the seasoned officer had taken it as a huge slight. He resented being overlooked for the leadership position and insisted he was the most qualified candidate. Even though he had come to respect the younger chief, he wasn't one to keep his thoughts or his criticism to himself.

Now that Chief deCordova was on sick leave, Perry had his chance in the limelight, and he was taking full advantage of it. With an ego as inflated as his waistline, the pompous man had wasted no time pointing out areas where he thought the chief was too lax. The lack of issuing citations had been his main complaint, but by no means his only one.

After thirty minutes of hearing the man rant and toot his own horn, Nate's blood boiled.

Perry naively believed that the threat of illegal drugs and organized crime was a thing of the past in The Sisters. A couple of years ago, a drug and gambling ring had been dismantled, and more recently, a parolee within the organization had been sent back to prison. Perry was hesitant to consider the possibility that a new threat had entered their community. He insisted that the drugs were only passing through the towns en route to their final destination. The Sisters, he believed, was still drug-free.

Worse, perhaps, was the fact that, if there should be a new problem, he had tunnel vision when it came to possible suspects. Otis Perry, with his high-handed ways and superior attitude, instructed the other three deputies not to waste valuable resources looking beyond the motorcycle gang as their main threat. He bragged about having run them out of town, even though they still stirred up minor problems in the area. There had been random sightings of them all over River County.

When Deputy Abraham pointed out that reported drug deals had increased in recent days, an angry Perry insisted they were 'alleged' deals with no solid evidence to back them up. His dogged determination to downplay the potential threat left his fellow deputies disgruntled.

Now, as they filed out of the station, the officers let off steam.

"Not just for his own health, but I hope the chief makes a speedy recovery!" Deputy Schimanski muttered. A twelve-year veteran with the force, Schimanski was a mild-mannered officer who seldom complained and was always eager to do as he was asked. He had worked alongside Otis the longest, and the two were friends. But even Schimanski had trouble with the way his friend was handling being in charge.

"You and me both!" Misty Abraham huffed. "A little bit of power has gone to that little man's head. He thinks he knows everything, but he's clearly an idiot!"

"What he lacks in common sense," Nate reasoned, "we're going to have to make up for. If he believes that only a motorcycle gang can be up to no good, he's lost touch with the world we live in." He looked at the man beside him. "Didn't you tell me that some of the most respectable business leaders in this town were the ones behind that big drug ring here in town?"

Schimanski nodded. "A bank president and a pharmacist. And I don't recall ever seeing either one of them on a bike."

Nate shook his head in disgust. "I don't care what

Perry says, we have to keep our eyes and ears open."

"You won't hear any of us arguing," Misty said. "I thought Vina's head might explode in there. She's as outraged as we are over his holier-than-thou attitude."

Vina Jones had been with the department for almost as long as Otis. She handled the responsibilities of desk sergeant, dispatcher, and defender of the law with ease. She was, Brash often insisted, the glue that held their department together. No one was sure of her exact age, but everyone dreaded the day she would eventually retire.

The three officers had reached the parking lot and their patrol cars. "He stuck me with patrolling the highway," Schimanski said, "but I don't know how many tickets I'll write. Unless someone is driving recklessly or at unsafe speeds, I have trouble justifying a stop just to pad the towns' pockets."

"You heard him." Misty sneered as she opened the door to her cruiser. "He hinted it could mean a raise for all of us, which is all he's worried about. Now we have to spend our days on traffic duty, just waiting for someone to go five miles over the speed limit or, Heaven forbid, roll through a stop sign. That, my friends, is crime stopping at its finest." She batted her heavily fringed eyes as she slid behind the wheel.

"At least you have the next couple of days off. That leaves me and Schimanski to do his bidding," Nate grumbled, heading for his own car.

He was still steaming as he opened the door. Neither town had an ordinance against parking on neighborhood streets, but Otis insisted it posed a threat. He said drivers had to swerve unnecessarily around the vehicles and could potentially cross into oncoming traffic. While the argument was theoretically possible, Nate had never seen heavy traffic on any of the towns' sleepy streets, including the ones in the downtown areas. All totaled, population between the two towns had yet to reach three thousand residents. Just as many people lived beyond the city limit signs, so there were times, of course, that traffic became congested. It was most notable at the beginning and end of the school day, or when there was a ballgame or event taking place. Like the police force and the fire department, the school district was consolidated between the two towns.

Ordinance or not, Otis wanted him to issue warnings to the owners of the vehicles and advise them to find alternative parking spots. There was nothing the police department could actually do to enforce the request, but Otis believed it was worthy of taking up the deputies' time.

As he started the cruiser's engine, Nate continued to complain. "Plus, I have to watch for littering and jaywalking, and issue citations to such hardened criminals. Like Misty said, crime fighting at its finest."

Despite misgivings, Nate dutifully drove through neighborhoods and downtown side streets, stopping when he saw a vehicle parked on the side of the pavement. He left a friendly note tucked beneath the windshield wipers. Otis hadn't told him to knock on doors to find the rightful owner, simply to issue a request for removal. He wouldn't waste valuable time arguing with perturbed owners when he had more pressing issues to attend. Issues like watching for stray gum wrappers on the sidewalks, or someone taking a shortcut across a deserted street.

Nate wondered how long this foolishness would last. According to Megan, her father wasn't cleared to come back to work for a few more weeks. He would be limited to desk work for several weeks after that, but at least the most qualified leader would be in control again. Nate had the utmost respect for Brash deCordova and was honored to serve under his tutelage.

Thoughts of the auburn-haired Megan brought a smile to the young officer's lips. They hadn't been seeing each other all that long, but the heart didn't measure affection according to a calendar. Nate was the first to admit he was completely smitten by his boss's spunky daughter. He was certain Megan could have her pick of boyfriends, so he thanked his lucky stars she had chosen him.

Turning onto Dickson Street in Naomi, Nate saw a car parked along the curb. Before he could pull in behind it, someone bailed out of the passenger's seat and took off at a run. He saw the person dart in and around cars parked in the driveway, before disappearing between two houses. Nate couldn't tell if it was a male or a female, but from their nimble build and the hoodie they wore, he assumed the person must still be in their teens.

At the same instant, the car shot away from the curb.

No matter how suspicious the person looked, running in itself wasn't a crime. Nate chose to let the young runner go while he pulled out after the car. Driving with busted taillights was definitely against the law.

He caught up with the battered Toyota in the next block. The driver pulled over and waited for him to approach, but he didn't roll down his window until Nate tapped on it.

The first words out of his mouth were defensive. "What are you stopping me for?"

"Are you aware that both of your taillights are out?"

"It, uh, it ain't my car." The man behind the wheel sounded nervous. "Belongs to a friend of mine."

"May I see your driver's license and proof of

insurance?"

"Why? I-I didn't do nothing wrong." His words were more of a whimper than a denial.

"It's required in every traffic stop."

While the man fished in his pocket for his wallet, Nate noted dirty, unkempt hair that hung to his shoulders. Beneath crooked and stained teeth, his Adam's apple bobbed up and down. The car was messy and littered with food wrappers, empty soda bottles, plastic bags, and a ratty-looking blanket, but Nate saw no evidence of a firearm or drug paraphernalia.

"What happened to your passenger?" Nate asked conversationally.

The man pretended not to understand. "Passenger?"

"Yeah. I saw someone jump out of your car back there. A friend of yours, I take it?"

"Uh, yeah. Yeah, man, a friend."

"What was her name?"

"Her?"

Seeing true confusion this time, Nate had discovered one morsel of information he needed. "What was his name?" he amended.

"We, uh, aren't that good of friends. I know him when I see him, but I don't know his name."

"But he was in your car."

"Yeah, we were just talking. Easier on his feet that way, you know?"

"Why did he run away when I pulled up?"

"We were done talking."

Ignoring the flimsy excuse, Nate repeated, "That driver's license and insurance card, please."

The man's hand shook as he transferred the items to the officer. According to his license, Timothy Boyle was twenty-five, which was the same age as Nate. His address was listed in nearby Cougar Springs.

"Mr. Boyle, would you mind stepping out of your vehicle and placing your hands on the roof of your car?"

"Wh-Why?"

"Because I asked you to."

Left with little choice, the man did as asked.

"Do you have any weapons on you, Mr. Boyle?"

"Uh, yeah. Pocketknife."

"No gun?"

"Why would I have a gun?"

"That would be my question, not yours."

"No gun, man. You can pat me down and see. Just a knife if my front pocket."

Once he was satisfied Boyle was telling the truth, Nate asked him to remain outside of his car while he verified his information.

His license and insurance came back good, but the car remained in question. The license plate was registered to someone named Leonard George, Jr.

"Who's car did you say this was?" Nate asked as he returned.

"My friend's."

"Your friend have a name, or is it like your runner friend back there?"

"No, man, the car belongs to Lenny. Lenny George."

His answer made sense. "And Lenny gave you permission to borrow his car?" Nate clarified.

"Yeah, yeah. Sure. Lenny told me to drive it."

"What kind of work do you do, Mr. Boyle?"

"Well, uh, nothing now, but I start a new job next week. At *Myrna's Meadows*."

"That new RV park at the edge of town?"

"Yeah, yeah. That's the one. I'll be mowing the lawn, keeping the place looking good, that sort of sh—stuff." He changed his wording when he remembered he was speaking to the law. "Can I go now?"

The man seemed unusually nervous, but Nate knew

that didn't automatically make him guilty of anything. Most people were nervous during a traffic stop.

"I have to issue you a ticket for driving without taillights, even if it's not your car. You need to talk to Lenny about getting those fixed."

"Uh, yeah. Yeah, of course. I'll talk to him."

Nate wrote out a citation. "Let me ask you something, Mr. Boyle. Have you heard anything around town about people selling illegal drugs?"

Timothy Boyle swallowed hard. He darted his eyes around, landing anywhere but on Nate's steady gaze.

"Dr-Drugs? I don't know nuthin' about drugs."

"You haven't heard anything on the street? None of your friends mention something about scoring a little weed, or maybe something harder?"

"N-N-N-No." The word came out in a stutter. "I, uh, don't got a lot of friends here. Mostly Lenny."

"What is it Lenny does for a living?"

"He's, like, a-a fixer guy at *Myrna's*. Got me a job there with him."

"He's in maintenance?"

"Yeah, yeah, that's it. Maintenance."

Nate pulled the top two copies of the ticket from his pad. "Here you are, Mr. Boyle. You're free to go now, but I advise you to go directly home and park the vehicle until your friend can get the taillights fixed. If not, we'll be issuing a second ticket."

Nate went back to his cruiser, watching as the other car pulled from the curb and drove away at a moderate speed. He knew he may not have a lengthy history as an officer of the law, but he did have good instincts. And instinct told him that something about Timothy Boyle was off.

On the surface, it had been a routine traffic stop. Despite driving without taillights, Boyle had a current driver's license, his insurance was in good standing, and the car hadn't been reported stolen. He was able to identify the owner of the car by name. He was nervous but not defiant.

But there was the issue of that youth who ran from Boyle's car, and the way he refused to look Nate in the eye when asked about drugs. When he emptied his pocket to show Nate his knife, a thick roll of bills had come out, too.

Nate's instincts told him that he had driven up on a drug deal.

After stewing over the incident, Nate brought it to Perry's attention.

"Acting Chief Perry, may I speak to you for a moment?" he asked.

Otis rocked back his chair. Vina had refused to let him use Brash's office, insisting that he remain at his own desk, among the other deputies.

"Yes, Stone, what do you want?" He made it sound like an imposition.

"I think I may have witnessed something this afternoon. I'd like your input on the situation."

Otis' manner made an abrupt change. The younger deputy came to him for advice. It was a nice change of pace. "Yes, yes. Have a seat, and tell me what's on your mind."

Nate pulled a chair from nearby and sat, but he didn't readily speak.

"Spit it out, Stone. I'm not getting younger here."

Knowing his suspicions wouldn't be well received, he was slow to relay them. "I think I may have seen a drug deal take place today." At the look of irritation crossing Perry's round face, he added, "I'd like your opinion."

"What makes you think it was a drug deal?"

"I came upon a vehicle parked along the side of Dickson Street. When—"

Otis jumped in and stopped him. "Did you issue a warning?"

"I would have, but as I pulled in behind the car, someone jumped from the front passenger side and took off running. I didn't get a good look at the face, but I'd say it was a teenage assailant wearing jeans and a hoodie. The car then pulled out in a hurry. I noticed that both taillights were out, at which time I pursued it and issued a citation for driving without proper taillights."

"Good, good. Very good. But where does the drug deal come in?"

"I believe it was taking place in the car."

"Did you see any drugs?"

"No, sir."

"Did you see money change hands?"

"Unfortunately, whatever happened took place before I arrived."

"Look, Stone, you're young and still wet behind the ears. Just because a person runs when he sees the police doesn't mean they broke the law."

"I realize that, Deputy Perry. But the driver, Timothy Boyle, acted suspicious. He was obviously nervous, and he wouldn't look me in the eye when I asked if he knew anything about drugs coming into town. Plus, there was a roll of money in his pocket. I think it may have been from the recent drop."

"Or from a recent paycheck."

"Boyle is currently unemployed."

"There are dozens of possibilities for him having money in his pocket. You need more than that to accuse someone of selling drugs."

Nate didn't back down. "Instinct tells me that Boyle

is hiding something."

"Instincts? What do you, fresh out of the academy, know about instinct?" A note of condemnation slipped into the senior deputy's voice.

"With all due respect, instinct doesn't just come from police training. We're all born with some degree of instinct, some more than others."

"And you think you're one of the people with higher instinctive skills?" He was now openly scornful.

Nate held his gaze. "As a matter of fact, I do."

"And what do your instincts tell you I think of your drug deal theory?"

"They tell me that you're highly skeptical, and that you have no intention of taking me seriously." Nate's straight-forward approach never quavered. "Which, quite frankly, doesn't make sense. Our sworn duty is to uphold the law and keep our community safe. Stopping a drug deal is the very definition of doing our duty."

Perry's face turned red. "Don't tell me what is and is not our duty. And don't usurp a superior's direct order, Stone. I am acting chief of this department. And I assigned you to traffic duty, nothing else."

"Are you saying you want us to concentrate solely on traffic duty, and turn a blind eye to any other crimes taking place?"

"Do not put words in my mouth!" Perry wagged a pudgy finger toward Nate. "Your orders were to issue warnings for vehicles parked along the street, to keep our sidewalks clean, and to watch for jaywalkers. Nowhere in those orders was mention of speculating on a supposed drug deal. Do I make myself clear?"

"Not really. If I do see a drug deal take place... you know, with a baggie or a pouch handed over in exchange for some cash... am I supposed to mind my own business and stick to the traffic detail, or do I pursue the criminals?"

"Don't be smart with me, young man!"

"I'm not trying to be smart. I'm trying to be clear. Am I, or am I not, supposed to carry out the duties of the law?"

Perry's face darkened to a deep scarlet. "Watch it, Stone, or you'll find yourself written up for insubordination."

"Again, Acting Chief Perry, I don't mean to be insubordinate. I'm just trying to determine what you expect of me."

"I expect you to stop chasing your own ideas and theories and to stick to your assignment!" Otis snapped.

Keeping his voice level, Nate clarified, "So, that means ignore actual crimes that take place?"

"That means make sure there is an actual crime taking place and not some off-the-wall theory of what may or may not be happening!" Otis thundered. "You're off the clock now, boy. Go home and think about what I said. Take orders from your superior officer, not from your gut."

5

Timothy Boyle's nerves were still on edge. The encounter with the deputy had shaken him up.

"They're on to us, I know they are," he lamented. He paced the small confines of the travel trailer, gripping the back of his neck with both hands. More than once, the points of his elbows banged against something in the narrow space. "I told Lenny I wasn't cut out for this. I told him, but he wouldn't listen!"

The door to the trailer opened. The newcomer stepped back quickly, clearly surprised to see unexpected company inside.

"Way to give a guy a heart attack, bro," he said to Timothy. "I didn't know you were here."

"Your car's parked outside."

"I can see that. I figured you dropped it off and got a ride back." He pushed past his friend, opened the small refrigerator, and pulled out a beer. "Want one?"

Timothy declined the offer. "Already had two."

With a deep scowl, Lenny popped the tab and downed a third of the beer in one long gulp. "You owe me for the beer, man." He dropped onto a lumpy couch that folded out into a bed.

"You owe me for taking your heat!" Timothy

countered. "I knew I shouldn't have listened to you. I knew something like this would happen."

Lenny leaned up in concern. "What happened? And stop pacing! You're making me nervous."

"Now you know how I feel. I almost got busted, man! All because I did you a favor."

"Don't tell me you messed this up. It was a simple drop, man. Deliver the goods, take the money, and come back here. Nothing complicated."

"Except that you have two busted taillights, and a cop pulled me over. I almost crapped my pants."

"Did the cop see you make the drop?"

"He saw the kid run, nothing more. I got out of there when he pulled up, but he followed me because of the lights." Timothy jerked the folding chair from beneath the table and took a seat. "He gave me a ticket. So now he has my name, my address, and my driver's license number. And you owe me for the ticket."

His friend's neck bugged out expectantly. "Speaking of owing..."

Timothy pulled a wad of bills from his pocket and threw it on the couch. In the tiny trailer, he barely had to stretch out his arm. "You owe me my cut, plus the ticket."

Lenny peeled off some bills and handed them to his friend. "Did the cop suspect anything?"

"I don't know. I was afraid to look him in the eye. Why didn't you just get your taillights fixed? None of this would have happened if you took care of your car."

"Says the guy who wrecked his two weeks ago." Crumbling the empty can in his hand, Lenny tossed it toward the overflowing trash can. It missed, landing beside a half dozen others like it. "Who was the cop?"

"Some young dude. I didn't catch his name. I was too busy trying to play it cool."

"In other words, you failed miserably, and the cop

saw right through your act."

"You don't know that. He asked if I knew about someone around here selling drugs, but he didn't finger me for it. He just went back to his car and drove off."

"At least that's something," Lenny grunted.

"Look, man. I did you a favor. I made your delivery, and I collected your cash. But I'm out. I don't want nothing else to do with this."

Lenny looked at his friend with a cunning look on his face. When he didn't speak, Timothy became nervous. He stood up, his movements clumsy. "I—I mean it. I'm done."

"Look in your hand, bro," Lenny said quietly. "There's an extra hundred bucks in there."

Timothy opened his palm and counted the bills.

"There's plenty more where that came from," Lenny told him. "Just play it cool, don't let the cops ruffle you, and do like I tell you. Everything's going to be fine."

"I—I don't know, man."

"Trust me. We're just the delivery guys. Do you even know what was in the package you delivered?"

"No. And I don't want to know!"

"Exactly. We're just couriers. We do what the clients ask us to do, which is to deliver their packages. We're like UPS, but without the brown trucks."

Timothy had to think about that for a moment. "You sure?" he asked after a while.

"I'm sure. Come on, man, I'll give you a ride home. And once you start working here, you may need to crash here with me until you can save enough dough to buy your own wheels." He looked pointedly at the cash in Timothy's hand. "With more jobs like that, it won't take long."

Timothy slowly nodded. "I like the sound of that." His smile revealed his lack of dental care.

"Then follow my lead." Lenny clapped his buddy on

the back. "Just follow my lead."

6

"I don't want to hear any arguments," Genny Montgomery said. "Granny Bert and I are coming to get you, and that's that. You need to get out for an afternoon."

"What about Brash?" Madison protested. "I can't just leave him to fend for himself."

"We're dropping Cutter off when we come. He can keep Brash company while we're out. Problem solved."

"What about the girls?"

"Mary Alice has them." She referred to her mother-in-law.

"Where are we going?" Madison asked.

Her best friend countered with, "Does it matter? You need a break. We're already on our way."

Knowing it was useless to argue, Madison didn't bother. Fifteen minutes later, she and Cutter had exchanged places, and Genny was pulling out of the gated driveway.

"Okay, where are you two taking me?" she asked.

"We're kidnapping you!" Genny grinned.

From the backseat, Granny Bert said, "Be glad we didn't blindfold you. I wanted to, but Genny said Otis Perry might see it and haul us both down to the station."

"Can you imagine how much pleasure he would get from that?" Madison mused. "None of us are his favorite people."

"He'd love nothing more than to throw me in jail," Genny confirmed, "so I nixed the idea of a blindfold."

"I, for one, am ever grateful, and not just because of Otis. I like to see where I'm going. Which begs the question... *where* are we going?"

"We thought you might like to see the newest additions to our little community," Genny answered.

"Oh, are we going to that little German restaurant, the one that took over the *Fresh Starts* building?" Madison asked.

"You mean *Oma and Opa's*? Cutter and I ate there one night. It was very good. But, no, that's not where we're going."

Granny Bert spoke from the backseat. "Hank and Virgie invited me to go there tomorrow night. If he's not busy with one of his buckle bunnies, I reckon Sticker will go along, too." Even after his eightieth birthday, Sticker Pierce could still turn heads. Granny Bert pretended the fact didn't bother her. "The owners are from New Braunfels, so they should know a thing or two about good German food."

Genny nodded. "We had the—"

Before her friend could finish, Madison broke in with an exasperated, "You two are killing me! Where are you taking me?"

"For the record, you obviously don't know the concept behind a proper kidnapping. The point is *not* knowing where you're being taken," Genny pointed out.

"No blindfold, so not a proper kidnapping," Madison argued back. "Tell me where we're going!"

"Remember when Myrna Lewis thought they were

going to build an interstate through The Sisters and bought some land and a couple of vacant buildings around here?" Genny asked.

"As if I could forget,"

"Part of what she bought was the old Tinkman place outside of Naomi. I'm sure you knew she was opening an RV park out there, but now, she's decided to expand. She recently put in a playground for kids and made hiking trails, and plans on enlarging the existing lake so that people can fish. And now, her latest brainstorm is to create a food truck park. She already has three or four steady vendors and is looking for more."

"Really?" Madison was clearly surprised. "I'd like to say good for her, but it is Myrna we're talking about..."

Myrna was a thorn in everyone's side, but she was particularly antagonistic toward Madison and her family. As Madison's best friend, Genny fell within her sights.

"Even though it served her right for being so underhanded, we all hated to see Dean saddled with that sort of debt from her greedy land grab," Granny Bert put in. "How such a nice man could be married to someone like Myrna is beyond me!"

"I know, but she must have some redeeming quality that only he can see. And it's a good use for the land, I must say. But a food truck park?"

Genny nodded as she drove through Naomi. "It's a smart alternative, you know, from owning a brick-and-mortar business. Less overhead, fewer employees, no upkeep on a building or dining room. And Myrna actually has a good idea. The trucks form a semi-circle around tables and benches and a built-in platform. I hear she's considering live entertainment."

"I know food trucks are all the rage these days. I just didn't expect a dedicated space for them here in The Sisters. That seems more like something for trendy, urban areas. Plus, I didn't know Myrna had a creative bone in her body, other than with her flower garden."

The woman was well-known for her meticulous lawn and colorful flower bed. Her overzealous obsession was legendary within the community. Unfortunately, she was also known for her very abrasive personality.

"Do you really think this will work out for her?" Madison asked.

"Her hothouse business didn't last long, that's for sure," Granny Bert said. "Having Myrna as a landlord doesn't bode well for this venture, either."

"At least she's made it look nice with all her flowers and landscaping," Genny admitted. "And I think you'll both be surprised when you see it in person."

Madison still looked skeptical. "I just pity the poor people who might accidentally breathe on one of her flowers! Remember, Myrna's been known to chase people with her hoe for committing such a sin." She chuckled at the memory of seeing the woman in motion. "Her and that little fanny pack of hers."

"If it's on her fanny, there's nothing little about it!" Granny Bert harrumphed.

Houses along the road became more sparse, and soon, they saw the signs advertising the RV park just ahead.

"*Myrna's Meadows.*" Granny Bert's voice held something akin to scorn. "Sounds just like a pompous name she'd come up with."

"I have to admit, though, it does have a nice entrance," Madison murmured.

Landscape timbers lined the entrance and guided cars inward, alongside a riot of colorful shrubs and flowers. The gravel driveway split around a large, lighted welcome sign.

The office was to the left and led to the RV spaces.

Each had a concrete pad with hookups and a small grassy patch to call its own. Six or so travel vehicles were already set up, most of them with canopies and outdoor chairs.

To the right were the food trucks. Like Genny said, there was a nice platform in front. It was currently empty, but all around it were tables and benches that could serve as either dining tables or concert seating. Strings of lights crisscrossed over the stage and among the tables. They were off now, but Madison imagined they would make a colorful statement at night.

There were three vendors parked in the semi-circle, with a fourth truck set further back. Two were actual trucks, one was a stationary food trailer, and one was an old school bus modified for mobile food service.

Only two cars were parked out front. The women's feet crunched across the gravel as they made their way across the parking lot.

"It's colorful, if nothing else," Granny Bert offered.

Benji's Barbecue trailer was black with western-themed accents, including red bandanna awnings. A simple blackboard listed the menu and pricing.

Beside it was *Toss Up*. A chopped lettuce graphic wrapped the entire food truck, almost lime green in color. Bright red tomatoes, orange carrots, and dark olives offered contrast. Their menu board was white, but the add-in options were listed in an array of vibrant colors.

The converted bus had a huge Texas flag painted on its sides; a single lone star in the patch of blue, with one white stripe and one red stripe flew beside it. The name *Texas Eats 'n Treats* was emblazoned on the overhead sign and was edged with neon lights. Instead of bullet points on their menu board, they used icons like bluebonnets, yellow roses, orangey-red Indian paintbrushes, green cacti, silver oil rigs, black horseshoes, and the like.

Their first stop was *Benji's Barbecue.*

"Why, Miss Bertha!" the man inside said with a smile. "How you doin', ma'am?"

"I'm fine, Benji," Granny Bert greeted him. "What about you?"

"Finer than a frog hair," he boasted.

"How's your mama and daddy?" Southern manners required that she ask about his family.

"Daddy's rheumatism is givin' him a fit, but Mama won't let him stop long enough to complain."

"No, I don't imagine she would," Granny Bert chuckled. She made a show of looking around their surroundings. "How's business doing out here?"

"We just set up last week, but we had a good turnout over the weekend. I'm takin' that as a good sign."

"Well, sign me up for two chopped beef sandwiches," Madison said.

"Benji, do you know my granddaughter Madison? And Genny Montgomery? Girls, this is Benji Prather. I've known his folks for longer than I can remember."

"It's good to see you again, Miz Genny. I've been so busy getting this set up, I haven't been in to the restaurant lately. And pleased to officially meet you, Miz deCordova. How's the chief doing? That was a sorry thing those folks did, attacking first responders like that. Seemed no one was safe. Firefighters, medics, police... It was a disgrace, that's what it was."

"I agree whole-heartedly. And Brash is healing, just not as quickly as he would like. Thanks for asking."

"He's a fine man, that Brash deCordova. Tell him I said hello."

"I'll do that. Oh, and no rush on those sandwiches. We're going to make a round, and I'll pick them up on the way back." Madison's hazel eyes twinkled with a smile. "Brash doesn't know it yet, but that's what I'm cooking for supper."

At the next truck, they found dozen of choices for salad. The main offering was a basic lettuce salad tossed with add-ins, but for protein options there was tuna or shrimp salad. The only other items on the menu were macaroni salad and one made of fruit.

With all its many colors, reading the menu was no small feat. While the women concentrated on keeping their eyes from crossing, another woman popped up at the previously empty window.

"Can I help you?" she asked. She looked to be in her early thirties and had streaks of purple, blue, and green throughout her bleached hair.

Madison wondered if her hair had inspired the menu board or vice versa. "This is our first time here," she said with a smile. "We're curious about what you have."

"Salad, salad, and more salad!" the woman replied cheerfully.

Madison knew her grandmother had an opinion on the woman's hair color. She also knew her grandmother was never shy about sharing her opinion, whether welcomed or not.

Genny shared the same concern and quickly spoke first. "How's business going so far?"

"I can't complain. Today's been slow, but the other days have been good."

Granny Bert let her personal commentary slide in favor of pumping the newcomer for information. "How'd you wind up in The Sisters? You're not from here, are you?"

"No. I'm originally from California and just kept moving east. First New Mexico, then Austin, and now here. My friend Lenny got a job here, so I thought, what the heck? Might as well go where the wind blows me."

"Your friends works around here, too?"

Her hair shimmered with color when she nodded. "The RV park. He's in maintenance. He told me the owner was looking for food vendors, so here I am."

"So, you've met the owner, have you?"

"Yeah, she's a little scary, to be honest." Remembering her manners, the younger woman straightened. "Oh. I'm Josie. Josie Bargus."

Madison decided to break up her grandmother's inquisition.

"I'm Madison deCordova, this is Genny Montgomery, and this is my grandmother, Bertha Cessna."

"It's a pleasure to me you ladies. Can I get you anything, or are you just checking things out for later?"

Madison hadn't planned to order, but Josie seemed friendly, and she did wish her business well. Impulsively, she ordered a salad to go with their barbecue sandwiches. Genny ordered the macaroni salad, saying her two-year-old girls liked anything with pasta.

With salad and change in hand, they waved goodbye and ventured to the converted school bus.

"I could easily gain ten pounds here," Madison commented as she read over the board. "Fried dill pickles, blooming onions, fried mac and cheese bites, loaded nachos, and taquitos. The boudin rolls and crawfish bites don't tempt me, but look at all those sweets."

"Fried Oreos and fried Twinkies?" Granny Bert asked skeptically.

"I'm seeing an overall fry-everything-in-sight theme going on here." Genny made a circular motion with her palm. "Not exactly heart healthy."

A voice spoke from behind them. "The pecan fudge isn't fried."

When they whirled around in surprise, a petite

woman smiled at them. "Sorry. I wasn't eavesdropping. Just pointing out we do have a few non-fried options, like three kinds of fudge, an assortment of cookies, and fried pies." She pulled a face. "Oh, wait. Those are fried, aren't they?"

Genny only smiled. She was rather famous for her apple turnovers, which didn't have to be fried. Cutter joked it was part of the reason he had married her.

"You work here?" Granny Bert asked.

"One of the perks of being the owner, I'm afraid," the woman said. "I'm Louisa. My husband Danny and I own this little slice of traveling paradise."

Granny Bert risked clogged arteries and bought a basket of fried pickles for them to share, with fried Oreos for dessert. They sat at one of the covered tables to eat.

"Not sure who she's trying to fool," Granny Bert harrumphed, "but that little gal selling all these Texas Eats is not from Texas."

"Why do you say that?" Genny asked.

"She called it pe-can fudge. Texans know that a pee can is something you take along on road trips, not something you bake with."

Madison reached for another pickle slice. "You do have a point."

From where she sat, she had a better view of the truck parked behind the others. It looked more like a mobile firework stand. With a large image of a bat in flight, it was identified as *The Vape Mobile.*

"Are you serious?" she gasped. Her tone was incredulous. "A vape shop? Are those even legal?"

"There's no city ordinance this far out," Granny Bert noted, "but the state definitely has their own rules and regulations."

"I can't see driving around selling e-cigarettes being legal, but maybe this is considered a permanent location," Madison guessed.

"I didn't know that was out here," Genny said. "I had heard three or four trucks, but I assumed they all served food, not... that!" She motioned toward the vape shop.

They chatted as they munched on the basket of fried pickles. When they were all gone, Granny Bert wiped grease from her fingers and reached for one of the cookies. "Here goes," she said. With an iffy expression, she determined, "Not as bad as I expected, but I'm not exactly a fan."

Madison had to agree. "If I'm eating fried desserts, I'll stick with donuts and sopapillas."

In agreement, all three brushed powdered sugar from their lips and pushed away the containers. With a smile, Granny Bert asked, "Well, girls? Is The Vape Mobile our next stop?"

Madison held up her hand like a stop sign. "I don't think so. That's one new business I don't plan to patronize."

"Ditto," Genny agreed.

"Looks like it may survive without your contribution, anyway." Granny Bert nodded to the two men standing in front of the sales window.

"I'd say you're right. And if those two are any indication, they have a rather varied customer base." One of the men wore the slouchy style favored by so many youths of the day. In contrast, the other wore a pair of slacks with a button-down shirt and tie.

"I just need to keep Wanda away from that place," her grandmother said. "Can you imagine the fun she would have? It looks like a fireworks stand, and that's what she would be like. A kid at a firework stand!"

"Heaven forbid," Genny murmured.

Madison agreed. "And knowing Miss Wanda, there might very well be an explosion!"

Friday nights in Naomi and Juliet lacked the vibrancy of those in larger towns and cities. Without a movie theater or entertainment center in either town, their kickoff to the weekend was mild in comparison to other places. Most of the teenagers went into Riverton or Bryan-College Station for fun. In contract, many of the young families and older generation went out to eat locally. But now, having more options on where to eat lent a festive air to the night.

Granny Bert and three of her friends were among the evening diners.

"Willkommen. Please come in." A plump woman wearing an apron and a friendly smile greeted the foursome as they shuffled into Oma and Opa's. "Table or booth?" she asked.

Virgie Adams answered for them all. "Better make it a table. We don't slide into booths as easily as we used to."

The woman's blue eyes twinkled in merriment. She couldn't have been more than ten years younger than the octogenarians. "Oh, don't I know that for a fact! I'm Emma Klein. Is this your first time to eat with us?"

"Sure is," Granny Bert confirmed. "I'm Bertha

Cessna. Welcome to The Sisters.”

“We’re the Adamses, Virgie and Hank.” Virgie made the introductions, while her husband stood behind her and offered a friendly nod.

“And I’m Sticker Pierce.”

Emma Klein took in the man’s monogrammed western shirt, starched jeans, and fine leather boots. His handsome, weathered face and handlebar mustache confirmed her suspicions.

“As in rodeo legend and western apparel king?” she asked.

“One and the same, I’m afraid.”

“Oh, my great-granddaughter will want an autograph! She’s a barrel racer and just loves your clothing line.”

“It will be my pleasure. I love seeing youth keep the sport alive.”

Sticker’s charming smile wasn’t lost on their hostess. A bit of a blush stained her rounded cheeks as she asked them to follow her.

Hank and Sticker held chairs for their ladies before taking a seat beside them at the four-top table.

“Any specials?” Hank wanted to know.

Emma rattled off two options. She left to fetch their drink orders, giving them time to decide what they wanted.

“They have a good selection,” Virgie said as she perused the menu. “Not just German food, either. I see chicken fried steak, burgers, salads, even grilled cheese sandwiches. You can never go wrong with grilled cheese.”

“I didn’t come to a German restaurant to get no grilled cheese,” her husband grumbled. “I want sausage and spaetzle.”

With a snort, Virgie chastised him. “You may as well order heartburn, because that’s exactly what you’ll get."

"You order your food. I'll order mine."

"Fine," she huffed. "But don't say I didn't warn you."

The other couple pretended not to notice the spat between their friends. It had been sixty years in the making and was now part of their daily life.

Sticker directed his question to his date, "What about you? What are you having?"

"I can't decide," Granny Bert answered. "The schnitzel sounds tempting, but so does the chicken fried steak."

"You know me. I'm a steak and potatoes man." Decision made, he closed his menu.

Emma came back with their drinks and a basket of warm bread made from scratch.

"Family recipe," she said with a wink.

Never missing an opportunity to gather information, Granny Bert struck up a conversation. "I hear you're from New Braunfels. What brought you to The Sisters? We're not exactly a hot spot on the map."

"No, but I remembered that TV show they made here a couple of years back about remodeling an old mansion, and I wanted to come by and see it for myself. While we were roaming around, we saw the 'For Rent' sign in this window and decided to take a chance."

"That was my granddaughter Madison in the show."

"That's why you look so familiar!" Emma gushed. "Oh, my. Two celebrities right here at one table. I may need both your signatures."

Granny Bert brushed off the flattery. "Mine's nothing but chicken scratch, and his isn't much better. But our fleeting fame on *Home Again's* remodeling show is old news. Why did you pick our little towns for your restaurant?"

Emma shrugged. "It looks like a nice enough place,

and my Leon needed something to keep him busy. Since I love to cook, I thought a restaurant would be just the ticket. Our brood has grown up and scattered, and this is somewhat of a central location between the seven of them. So, we figured, why not?"

After she had taken their orders and left, Virgie leaned inward over the table. "Would you just up and move to a strange town and decide to open a restaurant?"

Granny Bert harrumphed. "Of course not! I don't buy that story for one minute."

Hank stopped them with a groan. "Not again," he begged. "You two don't go stirring up trouble. That Miz Klein seems like a nice lady, and she makes a fine loaf of bread. If the rest of her cooking is anything like this, we need them to stay in business. Don't be making up rumors and driving them out of town."

"Who said anything about running them out of town? We just want to know their story and how they ended up here," his old friend told him.

Granny Bert and Hank were childhood friends and had practically grown up in the old mansion Emma spoke of. It was the very house where their parents had worked, and its secret passages had provided hours of fun for the mischievous children. Granny Bert had inherited the house from the childless matriarch of the town, Juliet Randolph Blakesly, and she sold it to her granddaughter when Madison's life had gone awry.

Unconvinced, Hank shook his head. "But I know you two. By the time you two sink your teeth into a story, you shake it plumb out of shape. You tell them, Sticker," he encouraged the other man.

The old cowboy held up his hands. "I'm sitting this one out. I've learned the hard way not to step in when Belle's on one of her rants. Besides," he said, sliding a sly eye to the woman he called his Belle, "I'm still trying to get her to marry me. I know when to keep my mouth shut."

"Apparently not, if you're still bringing up that old subject," Granny Bert sniffed. She turned her attention back to Virgie. "I wonder what her husband did before this. She said he needed something to keep him busy. Most folks their age take up gardening, or start a new hobby. Not many go out and start a new business. Especially not one in a town this size."

"Like it or not, the towns are growing, Belle," Sticker dared to point out.

"I never said I didn't like it. When I was the mayor of Juliet, I was always encouraging new businesses. Towns either grow, or they die. I just think it's curious that an elderly couple pulls up stakes and decides to put them down in a strange town. At that age, most people move closer to their doctors, not to a small community an hour away from the nearest hospital."

"And they sure don't open a restaurant," Virgie agreed. "Restaurants are hard work. It usually takes a few years for them to become profitable. It just seems unlikely that a couple their age would take on that sort of risk or that sort of workload."

"Maybe they're like you and Bertha, and like a challenge," Hank carped. "You two just up and decided you were some sort of private detectives at Madison's detective agency."

"I keep telling you, Hank, *In a Pinch* isn't a detective agency!" his wife corrected. "People just hire Maddy to do their snooping for them."

"And of course, you two have to pitch in and get in the middle of it. You're both too old for that sort of foolishness. One of these days, you're going to get hurt. You need to quit meddling in other people's business."

"Better than sitting in front of the television and turning into a couch potato," she shot back. "And we were talking about the Kleins, not me and Bertha. We grew up here. We have a reason to be here and a reason to worry about our community."

Granny Bert backed her up. "That's right. We welcome newcomers, but it doesn't mean we don't wonder about them." Her eyes wandered toward the kitchen. "And I, for one, wonder about Emma and Leon Klein."

Beneath colorful strands of lights, a newly erected sign identified the food truck park as 'The Grove.'

Nate opened the pickup door for his date. Stepping out into the night, Megan took his arm as they made their way across the gravel parking lot.

"I have to say, I'm impressed. I didn't know Myrna could pull off something like this."

"I take it you don't care for the owner?"

Megan hooted with unamused laughter. "Have you ever met Myrna Lewis?"

"Not that I know of."

"Oh, believe me. If you ever had the misfortune of meeting her, you wouldn't forget. She has absolutely no fashion sense whatsoever. Crazy colors that don't go together, unimaginative clothes that do nothing for her short, wide body, and she usually wears a fanny back around a waist you can't see but assume is there. It's black, like the crew socks she wears with her shorts."

Nate chuckled at the vivid picture she painted. "Sounds like a very colorful character."

"I see what you did there. Colorful, like her atrocious wardrobe. But that's only part of it. Inside her fanny pack is a full assortment of garden tools, including a pair of kitchen scissors. She gets down on her lawn and snips any uneven sprig of grass. I kid you not. She rolls around the entire yard like that."

"Seriously?"

"Seriously. And don't dare step on her lawn. More than once, she's tried pressing charges against someone for breaking off a flower blossom or trampling her grass. She's forever threatening people just for walking on the sidewalk. I don't think she's ever actually harmed anyone, except with that sharp tongue of hers."

"Surely, she's not that bad." Nate looked skeptical at the description.

"Ask anyone in town. She's bossy and bitter, and she doesn't have a nice word to say about anyone unless it somehow benefits her. Her voice, alone, will grate your nerves to shreds."

"That aside, it looks like she's got a nice place out here."

Megan had to agree. "I know, right? Weird. And totally out of character for Myrna Lewis."

They stopped to watch people milling about the food trailers and occupying tables around the platform. No band was performing, but a stereo blared music from several large speakers. A few couples had gotten up to dance. There wasn't a large crowd, but enough to be impressive.

"Let's see what they have to offer. I'm starved." Nate wound his arm around Megan's waist as they stepped forward.

They purchased a varied mix from all three vendors and found a table where they could eat.

"Not bad," Megan said, biting into the loaded tacos.

With his mouth full, Nate nodded and made a satisfied 'mmm' sound as he bit into a barbecued rib.

"I can see this being a popular spot," Megan said as they sampled more dishes. "I guess Myrna's not as clueless as I thought. Proof that wonders never cease."

"I suppose everyone has a good idea now and then. Shall I go back and pick us up some desserts?"

"Now that," the auburn-haired beauty grinned, "is a good idea."

"Anything in particular you want to try?"

"Surprise me. Just make sure it includes fudge and some of that peach cobbler from the barbecue trailer."

"Yes, ma'am," he said, dropping a kiss on her lips.

"Hey, Megan." A girl she had gone to high school with stopped by the table as Nate sauntered off. "Who's the hottie? Is he from around here?"

Megan had never been a fan of Miley Redmond, but she couldn't be rude to her. She actually felt sorry for the spoiled little rich girl whose father was in prison and whose mother ended up in psychiatric care, unfit to stand trial for her own crimes.

"Hey, Miley. His name is Nate Stone, and he's the newest deputy with The Sisters Police Department." Megan couldn't hide the proud smile playing across her lips.

"Just what we need. More cops," Miley mumbled. "The two of you looked awfully cozy. I guess you'll be breeding a whole new generation of cops."

Megan faked a bright smile. "You know what they say. Policemen and doctors are always in demand. Criminals and diseases never seem to go away." She looked at the two girls with Miley. "Hi. I don't think we've met before. I'm Megan deCordova."

"We know who you are." The dark-haired girl was as rude as Miley.

The other one offered an apologetic smile. "I'm Holly."

"Nice to meet you. I don't know about y'all, but this is my first time here. So far, I'm impressed."

"It's nothing like we have in Austin," Miley derided, "but I guess it'll do."

"That's right. You're going to the University of Texas. Do you like it?"

"Better than stupid Texas A & M." She all but spat the words, knowing it was Megan's school of choice. She held up her pinkie and her index finger, saying, "Hook 'em Horns." Bored with the conversation, she turned on her heels and said to her friends, "Come on, girls. No need to waste our time with a cop-loving Aggie."

Megan was more amused by Miley's behavior than she was offended. "Bye, Miley," she called to her retreating back. "Always interesting running into you. And nice to meet you, Holly and friend."

Only Holly returned the sentiment. "Bye. Nice to meet you, too." She was clearly embarrassed by her rude friends.

Megan waved to someone else she knew while she waited for Nate. He returned with his hands full.

"Oh, my word! What did you do? Buy every dessert there was?"

"Almost," he grinned. "Here's the cobbler you requested, and three kinds of fudge. Plus a half dozen fried options. Did you know you can fry a Twinkie?"

She looked at the dessert skeptically. "I do now."

They shared the different desserts, rating each one. They had a mild squabble over the winner, but Megan knew Nate's response was lackluster, at best.

"Nate?" she asked, touching his hand. "What's wrong?"

He hesitated for just a moment before brushing the question away. "Nothing. It's nothing."

"It doesn't sound like nothing. And that look on your face certainly doesn't look like nothing. Did something happen while you were gone?"

"Maybe it was all the sweets," he suggested, placing his free hand on his stomach.

Megan wasn't fooled. "You're avoiding my question. What happened?"

"It was…" He stopped before saying 'nothing' again. "Not a big deal. I just saw someone."

"That doesn't surprise me. I see a lot of someones."

"It was a guy I stopped recently for busted tail lights, okay? No biggie."

"Do you have this reaction every time you see someone you've stopped? Because my dad would tell you to toughen up," she teased.

"It's not like that."

"Then how is it? Because you're definitely distracted."

Nate didn't deny it. He simply said, "I don't want to drag you into police stuff."

"In case you haven't noticed, my father is a policeman. My boyfriend is a policeman. I'm sort of dragged into police stuff all the time. So, tell me what's wrong."

With a sigh, he confided in her. "I made a traffic stop the other day, but I suspected the guy was doing more than just driving without taillights. I think he was dealing."

"Really? Who was he?"

"He said his name was Timothy Boyle. His address was Cougar Springs, but he said he was starting a job here next week. He'll be cutting the grass."

"Here at Myrna's? Lord help him if he clips one of her flowerbeds!"

"That'll be the least of his worries. I think he's into something much deeper than grass." As an afterthought, he added, "No pun intended."

"Who was his customer?"

Nate shook his head. "I couldn't tell. They took off running the minute they saw me. I only got a glimpse of them from the back, but I'd say they were young.

Probably in their teens."

"Did you arrest this Boyle guy? Is he already out of jail?"

"I didn't actually see the drug deal, so I couldn't arrest him," Nate admitted. "But I'm pretty sure that's what happened."

"At least you have a suspect and know to keep an eye on him."

"Except that Perry wants me to do more important stuff, like warning people not to park on the side of the road or giving a ticket to anyone who drops a candy wrapper on the street. He'd rather I ignore actual crimes, so I can concentrate on his campaign to create more revenue."

Megan stifled a gasp. "He actually said that?"

"He refused to answer directly because he didn't like me using his own words against him. We left it with me ignoring my instincts and waiting for a real crime to occur."

"That doesn't make any sense."

"Tell me about it," Nate muttered.

"Otis Perry is such a jerk! He's always been jealous of Daddy, and now, this temporary power has gone to his head."

"We all tried to tell him there's a problem here, and that we can't just ignore it. But he's determined that if there are drugs here, it's because of the bike gang in town."

This time, her gasp wasn't stifled. "They're back again?"

Nate berated himself for speaking before he thought. He didn't want her to be worried. "There's been a couple of sightings in the area," he said, trying to play off his mistake. "Nothing to be concerned about. I only mentioned it because Perry is determined to pin everything on them."

Suddenly chilled, Megan hugged her arms. "Perry is an idiot. He has no business being in charge."

"I agree, but he has seniority. The mayor appointed him to take your father's place."

"For more than just his own sake," Megan murmured, "I wish my father would hurry and get well."

8

As a temporary work service, *In a Pinch* took odd jobs from around the surrounding area. Their primary clients were mom-and-pop businesses that had few or no employees other than the owners themselves. Sometimes, their clients were individuals who simply needed an extra hand. Despite his prissy ways, her sole employee was an excellent handyman. The fix-it-up jobs fell upon him, and Madison took most of the fill-in positions. And she definitely took charge of the more sensitive cases that required snooping. As much as she appreciated him, Derron Mullins was much too loose lipped to handle sensitive situations.

Due to Brash's injuries, their roles had changed somewhat over the past few weeks. Today, for instance, he was out on a job while she answered the phone and opened mail.

The first letter in the stack was propaganda and destined for the trash can, but the next one brought her up short. "What in the world!" she muttered. "Why am I still getting these?"

The letter was a remnant from the past. Like the others she had seen, it offered no return information. More curiously, it was addressed to *Grayson,*

McGarvey, and Associates, and it had found its way here, to Juliet.

Almost a decade ago, her late husband Grayson Reynolds and his friend McGarvey Ore formed an investment company. They thought it was genius to name the business after themselves but with a witty twist; they used their given names rather than surnames. Another stroke of genius, they claimed, was the fact that there were no associates other than their clients.

The partnership was long since defunct, but an occasional letter addressed to the firm still slipped through from time to time. Gray always shrugged it away as a random company using an old mailing list. Madison remembered one such letter arriving shortly after his fatal car accident. She had been knee-deep in shock at the time and had tossed it in the trash with only a cursory glance.

For reasons Madison couldn't explain, the rare correspondence had shown up again. Why the letters came *here* was a mystery within itself. The firm had been located in Dallas, and she hadn't moved back to her hometown until after Gray's death. Why—and how—had someone updated the firm's address to her current one?

Gray had always been vague about the details, but his former partner had gotten in some sort of trouble and spent a brief stint in the state penitentiary. It happened after they parted ways, both professionally and socially. Madison had long since lost track of McGarvey, and whatever wife he was now married to; she had known the first three. She sincerely doubted the man had kept up with her either, especially since he hadn't attended Gray's funeral. But who else could have updated the company's address to this one?

Curiosity had driven her to open the mysterious

envelope.

Now, another had arrived, and it was every bit as ambiguous as the first had been. It appeared to be a generic purchase order, the sort available anywhere that sold office supplies. Nothing identified the name or address of either party involved. What little information provided was written by hand, making the authenticity of the form even more suspicious.

The form had the usual columns for quantity, description, price, and unit. Few of the descriptions made sense to Madison, but something about the unit specifications suggested wholesale pricing. The problem with that assumption was that all the quantities ordered were extremely low. Single-digit low, in fact. Obviously, there was no minimum order required.

"What *is* this?" Madison wondered aloud. "And why did someone send this here?" She turned the paper over in her hands, looking for a clue. No matter how confounding the purchase order was to her, someone somewhere understood what it meant. Was there another Grayson and McGarvey she didn't know about? Someone here in the Brazos Valley, perhaps, with a similar zip code? It was the only explanation she could think of.

A quick internet search showed similar names but no exact match. She put in McGarvey Ore's name and hit search. Less than halfway down the page, she saw a familiar face. McGarvey had always been handsome with dark, wavy hair and a trim, lean physique. She hit the link to the story.

It was an old article about his trial and subsequent prison sentence. McGarvey had been found guilty for intent to sell an illegal substance. Due to his standing in the community and a spotless police record, he had served only a fraction of his sentence. The article was short and to the point. Madison suspected someone had arranged—or paid—to have names and certain details omitted.

There were only a few other mentions of Gray's old friend. Most were linked to his college days and early career. There was one article about the opening of *Reynolds, McGarvey and Associates*, a wedding announcement to Dallas socialite Patrice Hunt (wife #3), and mention of their divorce after his conviction. After that, it seemed that McGarvey had all but disappeared.

Was that how the letters found their way to her? Madison had to wonder. It still didn't make sense, but she had no other explanation. Grayson was deceased, McGarvey was MIA, and his ex-wife had long since moved on. Since Madison had been married to Grayson at the time of his death—it was a shell of a marriage by then, but legally, they were still husband and wife— maybe she was the only link to the company.

A company that folded a decade ago, Madison reminded herself.

One letter, she reasoned, could have been a fluke, but two seemed unlikely. Plus, this order was dated with last Saturday's date. It wasn't as if the letter had been floating through the postal universe for over a decade.

Who sent this, and what did it mean?

The nondescript envelope and generic form offered no clues. Not even the Houston postmark meant anything. Millions of pieces of mail went through their system every day, much of it transferred there from smaller facilities.

As she turned the envelope over in her hands, still searching for answer, her phone rang. Seeing Nate's name scroll across the screen, she answered with a smile.

"Hey, Mrs. D. How's your day going?" the young deputy asked.

"So far, so good. We're waiting for the physical therapist to arrive. And yours?"

"Not as good, I'm afraid. I wanted to talk to you about it, but I didn't realize you were waiting on company."

"He won't be here until an hour or so. I have time to talk. What's up?"

"I'd rather talk in person. Do you mind if I stop by your office?"

"Of course not. When would you like to come?"

His answer was somewhat sheepish. "Actually, I'm sitting outside your house."

"Oh. I didn't hear the gate." She was surprised the alarm system hadn't alerted her to his presence. Juliet Blakesly always had a wrought-iron fence around the estate, but when the *Home Again* team remodeled the old mansion, they had installed a first-class security system. "By all means, come on in. I'll go unlock the side door." Family and friends, the ones with the code to the private driveway, used the kitchen door to enter.

"No need. I'm in the parking area outside your office."

That explained why the alarm hadn't been activated, but she wondered about his use of the public entrance. Perhaps he didn't want to bother Brash.

"I'll see you in a minute," she said.

Her office occupied what was once the formal library. The stately old room, with its burled wood walls, newly painted accents, and a charming turret was the perfect way to keep her professional area separate from their living spaces. The two spaces were bridged by the seldom-used 'ladies parlor.' The library-turned-office even had its own door to the wrap-around porch. A newly added parking area made it convenient for clients to enter through the side gate and bypass the rest of the house.

Madison met him just as he stepped onto the lattice-edged porch. Nate was dressed in causal attire, marking him as off duty.

"This is a nice surprise." Madison smiled. She indicated the wooden rocking chairs nearby. "Would you rather sit outside or in?"

With a polite tip of his cap, Nate said, "We'd better go in. This is a business call."

He removed his cap as he stepped inside, releasing a headful of dark hair. With his strong jawline and wide-spaced eyes, he was more than Hollywood handsome. His face held character and genuine expression.

That expression was now one of concern. Instead of leading him to the cozy seating arrangement in the turret, Madison led the way to her desk, motioning him into one of the buttery-soft leather wing chairs. She took the other.

"That sounds a tad ominous," Madison said. "What's going on?"

"In two words? Otis Perry."

The sentiment was easy to understand. "Believe me," she told the young officer, "I get it. What has he done now?"

Nate ran his fingers through his hair. "It's more like what he hasn't done. He hasn't taken the rest of us officers seriously. All four of us—Vina and the three of us deputies—have told him there's a problem in town, but he blatantly ignores us."

"What kind of problem?"

Nate looked nervous, darting his eyes toward the wall. He knew about the secret passageways that ran throughout the house, and he knew one was directly behind that wall. Behind it was the guest suite that temporarily served as the master.

"He can't hear us in here," Madison assured him. "And if it's about the threat of drugs, I'm somewhat aware of the recent concerns."

"You are?"

She offered a smile and a 'what can I say' turn of her hands. "My grandmother is the information queen of both towns. My mother-in-law is the princess. If they say there's a problem, there's a problem."

"I wish Otis shared your reasoning, but he's too stubborn to consider anything other than his own opinion."

"And his opinion is that only the motorcycle gang can be responsible?"

"Exactly."

"What do you think, Nate?"

"I know I haven't been out of the academy all that long, but I think it's dangerous and irresponsible not to explore all possibilities. I know there was some trouble here in the past, but Otis seems to think with all that said and done, there's no one else to pose a threat other than bikers. I don't agree with him."

"And you've told him this?"

"Yes, ma'am. We all have. But he's not only determined we're overreacting, but he's also threatened to write me up for insubordination if I keep on about it."

"If I knew Brash wouldn't be even more determined to get back to work, I'd let him take care of it and put Otis in his place. Unfortunately, he's not physically ready for that yet."

"Which is why I came to you."

Madison cocked her head to one side. "I guess I don't understand."

"In no uncertain terms, Otis told all of us not to pursue other possible sources for what he called an *alleged* drug increase. But he never said anything about someone *else* pursing those options."

Her eyes widened in surprise. "Are you suggesting...." She turned a finger to herself.

"I am," he confirmed. "Thanks to Otis, my hands are tied. I'm too busy chasing his pet projects to do real police work. I've been forbidden to use department files or official databases to do background checks on persons of interest. I'm not allowed to tail a suspicious individual or to conduct a stakeout. I can't do anything until an actual crime has been committed. This goes against my grain, Mrs. D, knowing I should be doing something but not being allowed to do it." He locked his gaze with hers. "Since Otis won't let me do my job, I want to hire you to do it for me."

"If I get involved, Otis will have a cow!" It was the first thought that came to mind.

"Excuse me for saying this, but... I don't see the problem here." His tone was bland, but his blue eyes held a tease.

She laughed at his serious delivery. "I knew I liked you, Nate Stone!" Madison chuckled. "The thought of ruffling Otis Perry's feathers has never stopped me from anything before, and I don't see why it should now. But... I do have major questions. Who will I be watching? What am I looking for?"

"Good questions. Unfortunately, I don't have good answers for you. All we know—everyone, that is, except for Otis—is that drugs are coming into The Sisters, and that someone here is selling them. Honestly, we're probably talking about more than one dealer, so, until we can narrow it down, you may have your hands full."

"Surely, you have at least a couple of specific names for me. I can't keep my eye on every single resident in both towns!"

"I have a name or two, but that's about all." Nate

winced with the confession, "Like I said, you'll have your hands full."

She contemplated the ramifications of his proposal. Taking the job meant she wouldn't be here for Brash twenty-four-seven. He insisted that he didn't need a babysitter, but there were some things he couldn't manage on his own. However, there were more than enough people who could check on him in her absence, and he would be starting therapy next week. Surely, she could find time to squeeze in Nate's request.

"I can't promise results," she said after a moment, "and I'll have to work around Brash's schedule, but I think I can work in some low-level snooping."

"Anything is better than what we can do," Nate retorted.

"I'll need those names and what few leads you have, and I'll start to work as quickly as I can."

He pulled a piece of paper from his pocket and handed it to her. "I brought it with me."

Madison looked over the brief notes and short list of names. "You weren't kidding," she murmured. "You don't have much."

Brash's new therapist was Sid Adair, a big, burly man with a bald head and bulging muscles.

Madison met him at the front door with a smile. "It's so nice to meet you, Mr. Adair." She stood aside so he could wrestle two massive equipment bags through the door. "I take it you found the house without trouble?"

"It'd be hard to miss a house like this," he muttered. His eyes flickered to the impressive staircase. It was the centerpiece of the entry.

Madison did her best not to bristle, but she felt her

smile slip. His comment sounded almost like an insult. She made an effort to keep up friendly chatter as she led him through the stately old mansion. "Where are you from, Mr. Adair?" she asked conversationally.

"East Texas."

Well, then. That narrows it down to about the size of South Carolina. Very definitive.

She still made the effort. "The Piney Woods, or the coast?"

"You could say somewhere in between."

Still vague, but not that it mattered. She was simply trying to be polite. "What brought you to the Brazos Valley?"

"*Texas General* contracted the company I work for, so I'm here for the next three months."

"Oh, so you're like a traveling nurse?"

"You could say that."

"That must be interesting, moving around like that from place to place. I guess you get to see a lot of different places."

"Something like that."

Madison was thankful they had reached the back suite. The man had the personality of a prickly pear. She hoped he was better at his job than he was at conversation.

Entering the suite, she introduced the two men. "Sweetheart, this is Sid Adair. Mr. Adair, meet your new patient, Brash deCordova."

"Nice to meet you, Mr. Adair," Brash said, extending his hand for a handshake.

"Call me Sid," the therapist said. His manner was so starkly different from before, Madison's head jerked around. She had to make certain it was the same person speaking. "And it's a real pleasure to meet you," he went on. "I've followed your career since your college days. I rooted for you when you went pro, and again when you became a coach. You could say I'm a bit of a fan."

"I appreciate that, Sid."

The bald man pretended to look stern. "But don't think I'm going to take it easy on you just because I like you. I'm here to help you regain your full strength and mobility."

"I wouldn't expect anything less. I can take anything you throw at me. Even if it's not a football."

Madison listened in stunned amazement as the two exchanged pleasantries and a few laughs. *This* Sid Adair was nothing like the Sid Adair she had greeted at the door.

She broke into their conversation long enough to excuse herself. "I know the two of you have a lot to work on today, so I'll leave you to it. Can I get you anything before I go?"

"I can take it from here," the therapist assured her.

"We'll be fine, sweetheart," Brash assured her. "Even if you hear me squeal like a girl, don't worry. The first day of training is never pretty."

"Good luck then." Offering an encouraging smile, she blew him a kiss and left the men to their session.

9

Back in her office, Madison's fingers flew over her keyboard.

Aside from Granny Bert and Lydia, Madison found that social media was one of her best sources of information. Some people shared every aspect of their life online.

The first name on the list Timothy Boyle. Nate told her about the guy he stopped for a broken taillight. Something about him didn't feel right, especially how he was so unusually nervous.

According to the web, Timothy Boyle was twenty-five and single. His work history was varied, with entry-level jobs scattered in different towns and different professions. He had been a cook at *McDonald's*, a busboy at *Red Lobster*, car washer at *Suds 'n Shine*, dog walker for *Pet Palace*, and had worked at *Lawns Plus* and *Home Depot* for brief stints.

Timothy was an avid fan of graphic novels and on-line gaming. He also liked bars, bowling alleys, arcades, and movie theaters. He mostly shared other people's posts, but judging from the content and his own profile picture, he was hardly an altar boy.

Madison made a few notes and moved to the next

name on the list, Leonard 'Lenny' George. According to Nate, Lenny owned the car Timothy had been driving, and he had gotten him a job here in The Sisters.

The two friends were like the same picture, presented in black and white. Lenny hadn't worked in the exact places as Timothy, but his resume was just as scattered. He currently had one month of experience under his belt at *Myrna's Meadows*.

His idea of humor was a meme of a man being electrocuted while sticking a screwdriver into an electrical outlet. Which was unfortunate for him, since he was in the maintenance department.

The third name on the list was Gilbert Herrera, the only name Madison was somewhat familiar with. He had opened *Gilbert's Oil and Lube* out on the main highway about a year ago, and although Madison had never used his shop before, she had a feeling that might soon change.

Gilbert rarely used social media other than to advertise on his business page, but his girlfriend Terri made up for it. She posted all about their parties and their love of fast cars, motorcycles, and alcohol. Apparently, the couple felt the last three went hand in hand, even though Madison begged to differ.

She jotted down notes about his friends and places he frequented. She would follow up with a quick dive into his business details.

The last entry on Nate's list simply said 'motorcycle gang.' No names were attached.

Madison blew out a deep breath and shook her head with resignation. This wouldn't be easy.

She jotted down what scant facts she remembered about the men on bikes.

Multiple motorcycles, with one souped-up Camaro
Riders wore chains, spiked boots, leathers
Graphic tattoos

Run-in with Wanda Shanks
Stirring up trouble all across River County
NOT involved in first responder attacks
Beneath her notes, she wrote:
Why return? Recruiting new members? Pushing drugs? Or BOTH?
The possibility of either meant trouble.
The image of Granny Bert's tow sack floated through her mind.

As anticipated, Brash's physical therapy sessions left him exhausted. For the first several days, as soon as Sid left, Madison would help Brash into a hot shower, clean clothes, and bed. He was normally asleep before she left the room.

By the second week, Brash was adapting to the challenge, so Madison came up with what she thought was a brilliant plan. Though Brash was sleeping when she left, Lydia would check on her son while Madison had the oil changed in her Expedition.

After a hour plus of waiting, she wasn't so sure about the brilliant part. The mechanics at *Gilbert's Oil and Lube* still hadn't touched her vehicle.

The receptionist had suggested she make an appointment, but Madison said she didn't mind waiting. She thought it would give her a chance to scope out other customers and peek into everyday operations at the lube center. She was now regretting her hasty decision.

The waiting area had no view of the garage, the chairs were like sitting on a stone ledge, the coffee was burnt and bitter, and the only other customers were two elderly men. Neither could hear well, which meant Madison heard every word said between them. Rather than move closer to talk, the men remained across from one another and yelled back and forth. Madison had forgotten her earpods, so she had no choice but to listen.

After thoroughly discussing the weather, the prediction of a hard winter, and what it meant for cattle prices at the auction barn, the men discussed their families and what was happening at the VFW Hall. With those subjects exhausted, they moved on to gossip.

"Heard Melton Bishop's grandson got thrown in the slammer over the weekend," one of the men commented.

"That scrawny one with all them tattoos on his arms and neck?" It was more of an assumption than a question.

"That's the one."

"What'd he do this time? Wrap another car around a pole? All I can say is, the good Lord is watching over that boy. He's been in more scrapes than my wife's fender."

"Heard he had drugs in his system. Got caught over in Walker County, so he's locked up nice and tight."

"Closer to the state penitentiary," his friend grunted, "where he'll probably wind up. That boy's given his family nothing but grief."

"I hear he's been seen ridin' with a motorcycle gang."

Madison perked up, eager to hear what else he had to say.

"Melton called it a club but about a week ago, his wife saw one of the fellas he was with. She said he was a rough-looking character, like someone straight off a movie set. She didn't think no respectable club let members in looking like that."

"Otis Perry's been bragging about running those

cycles out of town. Guess he wasn't as convincing as he seems to think."

"You know Otis. He's always had a mighty high opinion of himself."

As they launched into tales of 'remember that time', Madison shot off a quick text to her grandmother.

Who is Melton Bishop's grandson?

Granny Bert soon replied.

Lazy overgrown kid named Robby. Picked up on drug charges over the weekend.

Madison knew she shouldn't be surprised that her grandmother knew about the incident. Somehow, she seemed to know everything that happened in The Sisters and to the people who lived here, even if it took place elsewhere.

Do you know if he's been riding with the motorcycle gang?

Granny Bert:

Wouldn't be surprised. I know Inez and Melton are worried about it. Inez saw one of the men. Said it was painted up with ink and had more chains than a pet store. Why?

Madison:

I'm at Gilbert's Oil and Lube. Two men in here talking about it. I think one's Herb Blackburn, not sure about other one.

Granny Bert:

Is he wearing blue suspenders and a hearing aid that beeps all the time?

Madison:

Sadly, no hearing aid at all.

Granny Bert:

Most likely Eddie Ray Burns. He and Melton are second cousins on his mother's side.

Madison shook her head, once again amazed at her grandmother's vast stores of information. The woman was better than any search engine.

Madison:

Know much about Gilbert Herrera?

Granny Bert:

Lived in Naomi about 5 years. Came from up around Dallas. Latest girlfriend is a live wire.

Madison:

Thx. Talk later.

Madison stood to stretch her legs. Seeing her car still parked where she left it, she went to the reception desk and asked, "Any idea how much longer it will be?"

"You're next in queue," the woman assured her as she popped her bubble gum.

"I think I'll step outside again for some fresh air."

After listening to the two old men yelling at one another for their entire conversation, the whir and grind coming from the garage bays was a welcome sound.

The first time Madison had gone outside, there had been too many vehicles in line to see inside the garage. Now, with only hers and one compact car waiting to be serviced, she could see somewhat better.

Gilbert's was a bustling place, with workers scurrying back and forth among the four bays. Madison didn't see the owner inside, but he could have been there; several of the men either had their backs to her or were half-hidden beneath a vehicle. She saw at least one woman in the signature red coveralls, her face as greasy and smudged as any of the men's.

Just before turning away to meander along the sidewalk, Madison saw the woman cautiously glance around the garage. Was she checking to see that no one was watching? Something about her sly manner felt suspicious. With no one else in clear sight, the woman walked over to a toolbox, took something from inside, and moved to the front of the car.

Madison couldn't see what happened next, but when the woman came back around the car, her hands were empty. A man in street clothes strolled into the open bay, and the woman gave him a slight nod. Another mechanic entered the space, and the two men started a conversation, occasionally motioning to the car.

The discreet exchange between the man and woman could have been a polite greeting, but Madison didn't think so.

She struck a pose and pretended to take a selfie. Instead, she snapped off a few pictures of the garage, trying to get a clear shot of the man in street clothes. She didn't see the woman any longer, but perhaps she would be back.

Madison whirled around when she heard a harsh voice behind her. It was decidedly female.

"What are you doing?"

Seeing the woman in the red coveralls glaring at her with fury, Madison came up with a quick reply. "Would you believe I've been waiting for over an hour to get the oil changed in my car? I was so happy with the service I've gotten here before, I wanted to post that it's worth the wait."

It was a huge lie, but she needed to come up with something. "Oh! I'd love to have a picture of us together! We can do it with the *Gilbert's* sign behind us. I'm so impressed you work here, you know." She kept up a constant chatter, maneuvering the woman into position before she quite knew what was happening. "I mean, most women don't make a career out of mechanic work. I think it's great, though. Say cheese!"

"I must look a mess," the woman murmured.

"No, but you do have a smudge here." Madison produced a tissue and wiped off a bit of grease before taking her place again. "Let do this again. Ready?" She snapped a shot. "Great. Got it." She had learned a thing or two from her grandmother, so she prodded for information in a friendly manner. "I don't think you were here last time. Are you new?"

"Uhm, yeah. I just started a couple of weeks ago."

"Really? Where did you live before that? Did you do this line of work there, too?"

"Yep, same thing over in Longview."

"How interesting."

The woman shrugged. "It pays the bills."

Madison wanted to ask more questions, but her phone rang. She glanced down at the caller ID. "Oh, sorry, I've got to get this. It was so nice meeting you... I'm sorry, I didn't catch your name."

"Jennifer."

The phone rang again, saving Madison from introducing herself. "Okay, bye, Jennifer." She flashed an apologetic smile while stabbing the button on her phone. "Hello?"

"I found out more on Robby Bishop," Granny Bert said.

"Great. Just give me one minute." She walked away from the building so that no one heard her conversation. "Okay, now I can talk."

Granny Bert launched right in. "According to Inez, he started seeing someone new about six weeks ago, and that's when things started going downhill. Now, mind you, Robby was never a saint, and his grandmother is the first to admit it. But this new woman introduced him to some rough characters, and he's started staying out all hours of the night."

"And his grandmother knows this *how*?"

"They have a loft apartment over the tractor shed, and Robby lives in it. He has to drive right past the house to get to it, and his car lights shine into their bedroom window. Inez says she hasn't slept well in at least a month. She said when those new rough-looking friends come in on their bikes, they make quite a ruckus."

"Motorcycles?"

"Yes, ma'am," Granny Bert confirmed. "Robby's trying to save up to buy one for himself, but now, he has to post his bail. Inez says they've bailed the boy out for the last time."

"How old is this Robby?"

"Too old to be considered a boy, that's for sure. I figure he's got to be pushing thirty by now."

"Definitely too old," Madison agreed. "How much does Inez know about the girlfriend?"

"Not much. Says she looks like she's been rode hard and put up wet."

"Do you know if Robby ever used drugs before, or is this the new girlfriend's influence?"

"I'm sure he's dabbled in them from time to time, but he's never been an addict. Inez says he's not one now, but she's worried he's headed that way. The girlfriend seems to be all for it."

"Wow. That's not good."

"Inez is worried sick, but Robby's a grown man. It's out of her hands."

"Okay, thanks for letting me know. I'm still here waiting on my oil change."

"Found out anything interesting so far?" Granny Bert wanted to know.

"Maybe. I saw something that looked suspicious, but I may have imagined it. I took some pictures, though, so I'll look through them when I get home. Nate said there was a strong possibility that something fishy was going on here."

"Keep your head low and don't get caught," her grandmother warned.

"It may be too late for that, but I think I covered well

enough."

"You're thinking on your feet. That's good. I taught you well. And I could use an oil change, too, if it helps."

"Thanks. It may come to that."

"I'll let you go. Hope you aren't there too much longer."

"While we were talking, they pulled my car onto the rack. Things should speed up now."

They said goodbye, and Madison walked back toward the building, her eyes on the garage. The man she had taken pictures of was on his way out of the parking lot. She took a quick picture of his license plate and sent it to Nate.

Keep your eyes open. Just left Gilbert's and looks suspicious. Fill you in later.

Nate was on *urban patrol* again, a new phrase coined by Acting Chief Otis Perry.

The name was preposterous, considering that, even when combined, the downtown areas of Juliet and Naomi could hardly be considered an urban area. Brash simply called it traffic duty.

When not in Otis' presence, Nate and the other deputies called it *vanity patrol* among themselves. It was nothing but an attempt to make Otis look good and to appear more competent and productive than the recovering head of the department.

Nate put his squad car in park at *New Beginnings.* He had been looking forward to a cup of hot coffee and one of Genny's specialized desserts all afternoon, but seeing a white car whiz through town changed his plans. He didn't have to clock its speed to know it broke the limit on a downtown street. Worse, it didn't bother stopping at the stop sign. A car approaching from the other direction had to honk and slam on its brakes to avoid a collision.

Throwing the gearshift in reverse, Nate hit his lights and siren. In this instance, he had no qualms about issuing a citation. Unlike a discarded candy wrapper, the driver's reckless behavior posed a legitimate concern for the public's safety.

Instead of stopping when Nate caught up to it, the car sped up. Nate followed close on its bumper. They wound through a residential neighborhood before leaving town on a blacktop road. At least there was less traffic, no pedestrians, and fewer chances of hurting the public out here.

Nate radioed dispatch to report the incident and to rattle off the license plate number. Vina informed him that Misty was finishing with a call at *Myrna's Meadows* and would cut the vehicle off when it approached. After running the plates, she came back and said the car had been reported stolen in LaGrange.

The white car had sped up to over eighty miles an hour. At this speed, Nate worried it wouldn't be able to stop at Misty's make-shift road block. He called ahead to warn the other officer.

As they made a curve, Nate let off the gas, but the white car wasn't as cautious. The driver saw it as a chance to outrun his pursuer, but he hadn't counted on a second police car sitting broadside in the road some fifty yards away. The man had only two choices—stop, or try to go around—and he chose the wrong one.

He didn't plan to give up now.

The moment his front tire hit the edge of the pavement, the hard jolt wrenched the steering wheel from the driver's hands. Grabbing hold again, he made a desperate attempt to stay on the road. He jerked hard to the left, sending the car into a tailspin.

Both officers helplessly watched as the white car

tipped onto its side, went into another spin, and did a complete flip. Another half roll, and it landed upside down in the middle of the road.

Nate and Misty scrambled to pull the driver from the mangled heap of metal. The driver side door was twisted inward, and the window was shattered. Nate tried opening the door, but it refused to budge. There wasn't enough clearance from the crushed roof to worm his body in or the driver's body out, so he ran around to the other side.

"I'm going in from the other side!" he told Misty.

"I smell gas!" she warned, already calling for an ambulance and more help.

The passenger side door already stood open, so Nate wiggled his way inside, heedless of the broken glass and trashed interior. The driver was half under the steering wheel, his face pressed into the roof of the car, which was now below them. Blood smeared his face and arms, but he was alive.

"Sir! Sir, can you hear me?" Nate screamed.

There was a barely audible reply.

"Good. That's good. I'm going to get you out of here, but I need your help. Can you do that? Can you help me get you to safety?"

"T—Try," he man whispered.

"Good. Now, try to give me your hand. I know it's going to hurt, but I'm going to pull you free of the steering wheel. Then we're going to crawl out of here, okay? Nice and steady. Now, give me your hand."

It was a long, excruciating process, but Nate finally disentangled the man from the wreckage. Once free, the driver was clinging to consciousness and unable to stand, much less walk, so Nate and Misty half-pulled, half-dragged him a safe distance away. They had him laid out in the grass when the ambulance arrived.

It wasn't until much later that Nate saw the text

from Madison.
It was the same car she had told him to watch for.

10

Extricating the driver from such wreckage left Nate with a bandaged hand, but it was far better than the other man's injuries. The driver had a severe concussion, several broken bones, a shattered elbow, and internal bleeding. He was airlifted to one of Houston's best trauma units.

Nate stopped by Madison's office to give her an update. "His name is Damien Cotulla," he said. "The car was stolen from a driveway in LaGrange a week ago while the owner was out of town. When the woman returned and discovered it gone, she immediately reported it to the police."

"Why would a man take a stolen car to a mechanic shop to have his oil changed?"

"We don't know for certain that Cotulla was the one to steal the vehicle. He could have bought it, not realizing it was stolen."

"But he ran from you when you turned on your lights and siren. That doesn't suggest innocence."

"He could have been running for other reasons," Nate pointed out. "Unfortunately, we haven't been able to question him yet. He underwent surgery and is still listed in serious condition."

"I don't suppose you found drugs at the scene?"

He shook his dark head. "TV makes it look excruciatingly thorough. They account for each scrap and morsel, but it doesn't work like that in real life. The scene was a complete mess, but that I'm aware of, no drugs were found."

Madison twirled the pen in her fingers like a baton. After a moment of thought, she said, "Stolen car or not, I think I have an idea of why this Damien Cotulla went to the oil center."

"Great. I'm listening."

"I saw something strange happen. A female mechanic was in one of the bays, and I noticed her looking around, like seeing if the coast was clear. Then, she went over to a toolbox, put something in her hand, and mosied up to the hood of the car. When she came back around, her hands were swinging loosely by her side. There was nothing in either hand, which meant she left whatever it was there."

"And you believe it wasn't a tool of some sort or an oil filter?"

Madison shook her head. "No, I don't. It wasn't very large, or I would have seen it. It was small enough to put in the palm of her hand. She was overly casual, if you know what I mean. But the most telling thing was that this Damien guy walked into the bay, and she gave him the tiniest of nods. Another mechanic came in and started talking to the guy. I took the picture when the car left."

"Any idea of who this woman is?"

With a playful smile, Madison said, "I'm not Bertha Cessna's granddaughter for nothing. She trained me well when it comes to getting information from people. The woman's name is Jennifer, she moved here from Longview, and this is what she looks like."

Nate gaped when she handed him her phone. "You

took a picture with her?"

"It was the first thing I could think of. I guess she saw me watching the bays. She slipped up behind me and demanded to know what I was doing. I made up something about being impressed with a woman in that line of work and asked if I could take a picture with her. I pretended to be a steady customer and wanted to share a good review on social media. She was too dazed to object."

The young officer chuckled. "All I can say is, you learned from the best. I've seen your grandmother in action, mainly when she drilled me for information about dating her great-granddaughter. Or I guess step great-granddaughter."

"You had it right the first time. We're all one big, happy family."

"Mind if I send this photo to my phone?"

"Of course not. That's one reason I took it."

"Perfect." He transferred the photo and returned her phone. "Thanks, Mrs. D. I'll check her out. I may not be able to run a background check without Otis breathing down my neck, but I'll do what I can." He looked a bit sheepish when he asked, "Did you find anything on those names I gave you?"

"Not yet, but I'm still working on them."

"I understand. I know I didn't have much to give you."

"Something is better than nothing. The motorcycle gang, however..."

"I know. Unless they come back—which I hope they don't—we can't find out names or anything."

"And if they don't come back," Madison pointed the obvious, "then clearly they aren't the problem."

"Exactly." Nate stood and thanked her again for her help. "If he's up to it, I'd like to go in and say hello to the chief."

"He'd love that. I'll walk with you."

"You're welcome to, of course, but I'm sure you have things to do. I can see myself in if you prefer. I don't think I'll get lost on the way there, even though this is a big house." He smiled.

"If you do get lost," she teased, "just holler, and I'll come looking for you."

"Here you go, dollface." Derron Mullins sashayed into the office and delivered the day's mail to Madison's desk.

She looked up from her computer monitor. "Thanks. Are you through building those shelves for Carson Elliot?"

"All done. And guess what?" he asked, his eyes twinkling with delight. He didn't give her time to respond. He couldn't wait to blurt out, "I'm going to take dancing lessons from him!" Derron twirled and did a smooth glide around the room. "I know he's older, but the man is absolutely dreamy. And he's so graceful." He twirled again.

Madison wasn't surprised that Derron was temporarily infatuated with the older man. She didn't have the heart to tell him the dancer wasn't gay; he would find that out soon enough. With the attention of an eight-year-old, Derron would be distracted by some shiny bauble or some other handsome face, and all traces of heartache would be erased.

Smiling, she simply agreed with him. "Yes, Carson is very talented."

Humming a waltz, Derron danced his way over to his desk. The piece wasn't a fine antique like hers, but rather an excellent, scaled-down replica. By the time Derron came down out of the clouds, Madison had already opened most of her mail.

When she saw the letter with no return address, she knew it would be addressed to *Grayson, McGarvey, and Associates.* Puffing her cheeks with a sigh, she slid the letter cutter beneath its flap and took out an all-too familiar purchase order.

Still no names. Still confusing descriptions. Someone, for instance, had ordered one six-pack of Special, and one single Special. They also ordered four two-ounce portions of Tumblers.

All the tumblers she had ever seen held much more than two ounces.

The rest of the order was much of the same. Simple but unconventional product descriptions. Low quantities of items, many of them written on different lines. Instead of adding the total number together, the order was written as one unit of MultiMix: Red, two units of MultiMix: Red, and then three units of MultiMix: Red. Wouldn't it have been easier to simply note it as six? There were similar entries on other products, too, including a MultiMix: Blue, Straws, and Pouches.

"It must be some sort of wholesale warehouse, the kind open to store owners. Maybe it was written down as the customer selected it?" she mused. "Maybe they decided one or two wasn't enough and kept adding more?"

Derron heard her mumbling from across the room. "What's that, dollface?" he asked, swiveling his chair around to face her.

"Oh, nothing. Just a confusing purchase order."

"What did you order? I restocked all our paper supplies last week."

"Actually, this isn't mine. I keep getting someone else's mail."

"And you opened it? Isn't that illegal?" He squinted

at her through narrowed eyes.

"It's addressed to Gray, actually. I wasn't a part of that particular venture but his estate went to me, so in a roundabout way, I suppose I'm opening my own mail," she reasoned.

"Okay, then. Enjoy." He twirled back around, lost in his own world.

Madison looked back at the letter in her hand. None of it made any sense. Not the purchase orders themselves, nor the fact she received them.

She was still confused about it that evening.

Halfway through dinner, Brash said, "You may as well tell me."

Her first thought was that he had heard about the drugs in town and the shambles Otis was making of the investigation. Or, according to Nate, the non-investigation.

"Tell you what?"

"Whatever it is that's bothering you. You're clearly distracted."

"I'm sorry, sweetheart. Did you say something, and I missed it?"

"No. I just know that look on your beautiful face. Something has you either upset, worried, or both. Is it this new case you're working on?"

Due to his job as an officer of the law and her tendency to skirt around it when helping some of her clients, they had agreed that the fewer details he knew, the better. And while she was hardly a doctor or lawyer, Madison referred to her jobs as a 'case' and tried to offer her clients the same manner of confidentiality. If need be, she gave her husband only a condensed version of compromising assignments.

"No, this isn't about the job."

He looked at her expectantly, but she offered no explanation. "Are you going to keep me in suspense, or are you going to tell me what's bothering you?"

Madison pushed the food around on her plate. "You know that Gray and I had our own firm, *Reynolds Investments*. It grew at a steady pace and was doing quite well until his parents—okay, mostly his mother— pushed him to *Go Big*." She mimicked an explosion with her hands. "You also know that when he died and left the firm heavily in debt, they bailed it out. They couldn't have their son's good name besmirched." A bitter note slipped into her voice. "Unfortunately, that goodwill didn't extend to me and our personal finances. I had to dig my own way out of that one, even though Gray was the one to bury us. Charles and Annette wouldn't—" She stopped abruptly, catching herself in the middle of an old grudge. "Scratch that. Annette has finally made amends for the damage she caused, and I need to be more gracious. Most days, I do just fine. But then there are times when it all comes back in vivid color... Anyway, this isn't about *Reynolds Investments*."

"Okay." He patiently waited for her to tell him what it *was* about.

"Did I ever tell you that, before we opened our firm, Gray opened a small one with a friend of his from college?"

"No, I don't think you ever mentioned it."

"Probably because it was hardly worthy mentioning. Both Gray and McGarvey Orr had promising careers with big corporations, but they wanted to start something of their own. So they formed a small investment company and called it *Grayson, McGarvey, and Associates*."

"Clever," Brash said. "They used their first names rather than last."

"They thought so."

"And the *Associates*?"

"They thought that was the most clever part of all. Their so-called 'associates' were their clients." Her mouth twisted with a wry expression. "What few there were, anyway. They folded just over a year later."

"How long ago was this?"

"Let's see..." She calculated dates in her head, connecting them to events in their lives. "It had to have been well over ten years ago. A few times while Gray was still alive, we would get occasional mail addressed to the firm. We didn't think much of it. We figured someone had probably wasted their money on an old mailing list. But then, the weirdest thing happened."

"What's that?"

"A letter addressed to *Grayson and McGarvey* came here. To Juliet."

Brash looked as perplexed as she felt. "How did that happen?"

"I have no idea. After the firm closed and after we drifted apart socially, McGarvey was accused of intent to sell illegal drugs. There wasn't concrete evidence against him, but the DA made a convincing case based on circumstantial evidence. He served a portion of his prison sentence, but it cost him everything. His career, his latest wife, and most of his friends. According to what I found on the internet, he dropped off the radar at that point. I'm assuming he didn't leave a forwarding address. And, of course, you know Gray died in a car accident. I suppose if a letter was mailed to our old Dallas address, it was forwarded here to Juliet."

"It wouldn't be after all this time. Forwarding services don't last more than a year unless you pay to extend that time. I believe another eighteen months is the max. When did you get the first letter here?"

"About three weeks ago. Today, I received the third one."

"Persistent, aren't they?" he murmured.

"If you promise not to arrest me, I'll admit that I opened them. Consider me one of the *Associates*."

"I'm currently on sick leave, so you're safe with me." His dark eyes twinkled as he added, "Just as long as Otis doesn't get wind of your reckless disregard for the law."

Madison rolled her eyes. "Isn't that the truth!"

"What did the letter say?"

"That's the really strange thing. They're not letters. They're more like purchase orders, but not like any I've ever seen."

"What do you mean?"

"Hold on, I have one in the kitchen. I'll be right back. Need anything while I'm in there?"

"You can take my plate, if you will."

Loading the tray with their dishes and carrying it to the kitchen, she returned with one of the strange correspondences.

Brash looked it over curiously. Frowning, he agreed with her earlier assessment. "You're right. These are strange."

"I know, right? What do they mean? I can't begin to imagine what a two-ounce tumbler looks like!"

"I always thought the name tumbler implied they were over-sized and likely to tumble over."

"I did, too," Madison said. "So, what's this two ounces mean? It's all very strange, if you ask me."

"If you get another one, please let me know."

"I will. I'd send them back, but not a single one of them includes a return address. I remember the ones mailed to our old address didn't, either. That was another thing that always struck me as odd."

Brash looked thoughtful. "How well did you know this McGarvey fella?"

"About as well as I know some of your football buddies?" she suggested. "First-name basis, friendly enough to hug and say hello if we run into each other somewhere, but not much beyond that. I went to two of McGarvey's weddings and sympathized with the jilted first wife. Gray and I didn't go to his trial, and McGarvey didn't come to Gray's funeral. Honestly, I haven't thought about him in years."

"What did Gray say about the charges against his old friend?"

"Not much, as I remember. He didn't seem too concerned about it. He said McGarvey always came out on top, and he didn't see why this time would be any different. He was understandably upset when McGarvey was found guilty and sent to prison."

"I imagine so."

"What are you thinking? I see those wheels turning."

"I don't know enough about the situation to think much of anything. Do you mind if I do a little digging into this McGarvey fellow? What did you say his last name is?"

"Orr. O-R-R. And no, I don't mind at all. I'd like to know what became of him. Mostly, though, I want to know why I'm getting mail meant for a firm that went out of business years ago. And here, of all places! Gray has no connection at all to my hometown."

"That's a very good question," Brash said with a thoughtful expression. "Very good, indeed."

11

"Sybil and I are headed over to *Oma and Opa's* for streusel," Granny Bert informed her granddaughter over the phone. "Come join us."

"That sounds nice, but I'm not sure this is a good time," Madison answered.

"Why not? I know how well you like streusel."

"Well, uh, the therapist is here."

"And?" her grandmother demanded.

"And I'm always here when he is."

"Do you help him with the sessions?"

"No, ma'am."

"Then, why do you need to be there?"

Madison was hesitant to put it into words. She didn't particularly care for the man, even though he came highly recommended. She had no reason not to trust him, yet something nagged at the back of her conscience. With Brash relegated to the back bedroom, Sid Adair could have the run of the house and, for once, her husband would be none the wiser.

She made a lame excuse that quickly petered out. "It's just that..."

"This won't take long, but I think you'll want to hear what we have to say."

"Okay," she decided, "but I can't stay long."

"We'll save you a seat."

It was mid-morning, so the café wasn't busy when Madison stepped inside. She easily spotted the two elderly women and the promised empty chair.

"You seemed to be in a hurry, so I ordered for you," her grandmother said in her normal take-charge fashion.

The other woman greeted her with a smile. "Hello, Madison, dear."

"Hey, Miss Sybil."

"How's Brash doing?" Granny Bert's oldest and dearest friend wanted to know.

"The physical therapy sessions are tough, but he's taking them like a pro."

"I'll try to get around next week and say hello."

Madison responded with a warm smile. "I'm sure he'd like that."

Without preamble, Granny Bert announced, "Sybil and I have reports to share with you."

Madison didn't dare smile. Leave it to her grandmother to refer to gossip as *reports*.

"Oh?" she asked simply.

"You start, Sybil," Granny Bert encouraged her friend.

"Well, you know how Lula Mae Jones insists that her family always gathers for Sunday dinner."

She didn't, but Madison nodded just the same.

"She swears that last week, her great-grandson was higher than a kite. Had a goofy look on his face and was all fumble fingers. He even spilled gravy on her best tablecloth." She nodded as if that, in itself, was definitive proof.

"Is that the kid with thick glasses and pimples? Shawn, I think his name is? He was on the baseball team the first year Blake played," Madison recalled.

"He quit halfway through the season."

"LaShawn," she corrected. "You know I don't like to talk ill about folks, but Lula Mae says he takes after his father and is too lazy to finish anything he starts. Now, she's worried he's mixed up with drugs, and she's beside herself, fretting over it."

"Is this the first time he's done something like this?" Madison knew that often, even parents were oblivious to their child's drug use. Grandparents and great-grandparents were even more prone to miss the signs.

"She didn't say, but I figure not. She seemed pretty sure about it."

Madison pulled a small notebook from her purse and jotted down a note. "What's LaShawn's last name?"

"Golden."

"That's not all," Miss Sybil continued. "A couple of his friends were expelled from school last week for bringing unmarked pills to school."

"That is worrisome," Madison agreed with a frown.

"According to some of my sources," Granny Bert pitched in, "there's been some strange activity late at night. Neighborhood watch groups say there's been more traffic on their streets after dark, and some swear they've seen drug deals going down."

An apron-bedecked woman brought a tray to their table, interrupting their conversation.

"Here you ladies are. Three streusels with three cups of freshly brewed coffee."

Granny Bert made the introductions. "Emma, this is my granddaughter Madison. Madison, this is *Oma* herself, Emma Klein."

"A pleasure to meet you! *Willkommen.*"

"Yes, it's very nice to meet you, too," Madison said. "And I'm so glad we have a new restaurant to fill this space."

"I took one look at it and told my Leon we should move here and open up a restaurant."

"Just like that?"

"Just like that!" she announced proudly. Belatedly, she made the connection who Madison was. "Oh! You're her! You're the one they made the show about. The one who remodeled the house."

"I didn't do much of the remodel. That was all *Home Again*," Madison said modestly.

"Well, I enjoyed it immensely. That's what brought us to town, actually."

"Really? No one's done that in a while. When the show first aired, of course, the town was swarming with sightseers, but that became old news real fast. On to bigger and better things, so to speak. But I'm glad you remembered us."

"Oh, I was a big fan of the show." Her cheeks suddenly colored. "Listen to me, carrying on like an old fool. I'll let you ladies enjoy your desserts." She moved to another table, fussing over the napkin container.

"Like I was saying," Granny Bert said, leaning in to continue their conversation, "there's been some unusual traffic in town. Unfamiliar faces at the gas stations or at the laundromat and the grocery store. I'm hearing all kinds of reports about strangers in town."

"Maybe we're growing. After all, the Kleins moved here."

"Don't you find that a bit strange, too?"

At her grandmother's pointed question, a line appeared across Madison's forehead. "A bit. I didn't realize our towns could inspire such a spontaneous reaction like that. But maybe that's what's happening. People are tired of the city and are looking for a slower lifestyle."

"I haven't heard of that many houses being sold or built in the area," Granny Bert contradicted. "In fact, I heard the real estate market has been more sluggish than normal."

The line on Madison's forehead deepened. "Then where are all these strangers coming from?"

"That's what I want to know," Granny Bert answered.

"This streusel is delicious," Sybil said. "I wonder if I could get her recipe."

"I doubt it," her friend harrumphed. "She wants you to buy hers, not make your own."

"True." She took another bite. "Oh! Did I tell you about Dorothy McNutt?"

The question was directed toward Madison. "I don't think so. Who's Dorothy McNutt?"

"Her family's from Cougar Springs, but they moved in a little closer to Naomi a few years ago. Anyway, she found a wad of money in her daughter's purse. She insists the girl either stole it or has a side job that pays a lot better than her job at the school cafeteria."

Madison narrowed her eyes. "How old is this girl of hers?"

"Oh, I'd say about forty. Wouldn't you think so, Bertha?" She consulted her friend.

"At least that."

"Wait." Madison had trouble with the story. "Why was someone going through their forty-year-old daughter's purse? I didn't even do that to Bethani when she was fourteen!"

"If you knew Dorothy's daughter, you might understand," was all Miss Sybil would say.

Granny Bert had no trouble speaking her mind. "What Sybil won't say is that this girl has been in trouble before. Her fingers are a little tacky, if you know what I mean. Dorothy tries to keep her in line, but Carly can be a handful. And for once, she doesn't think Carly stole the money."

Madison leaned across the table, keeping her voice low. "She think she's selling drugs?"

"Dorothy didn't say it in those words," Granny Bert admitted, "but I am. I suspect that's exactly what Carly is doing."

Madison glanced up to see Emma Klein still dawdling nearby. When the other woman realized she was caught, she flushed and moved quickly away, but not before Madison flashed her a smile.

During the height of the remodeling show, Madison had more than her share of admirers. It came with the territory, she supposed, but she had almost forgotten how intrusive it could be. Only the worst encounters still lingered in her mind.

Madison redirected her attention to the subject at hand. "Do you think there's a connection?" she asked. "Carly works at school, and this is at least three kids who've been caught with drugs recently."

"I hadn't thought of that, but you're right. It would be easy to slip a little something extra on their lunch trays, wouldn't it?" Granny Bert mused.

Her eyes narrowed in thought, Madison wondered, "Who do we know that works in the school cafeteria? Someone we can trust to watch for that kind of thing?"

Granny Bert never missed a beat. She answered almost immediately. "Joyce Williams. She's in one of my Bunco groups. I know she'll help us."

"Good. That may give us a few leads on that end. Anything else you've heard around town?"

"Wanda insists she saw a drug deal take place outside of *Montelongo's* Friday night," Miss Sybil said, "but I'm not as convinced. We went in time for the early bird half-price margaritas special, and she wanted her money's worth. I had a heck of a time getting her out of there on my own. Once we finally made it to the parking lot, a young man in a beat-up Toyota pulled up to the curb, and two girls walked over to him. Wanda insists they were buying drugs, but I'm not so sure. The way they were giggling and flirting, I figured they were exchanging phone numbers."

"Did you see them passing something between them?"

Sybil nodded. "It looked like the guy offered his first, and then one of the girls gave him hers. Wanda wanted to get close enough to hear what they were saying, but she stumbled on the curb and hit the hood of a car, which set off the alarm. The Toyota shot out of there like it was on fire, and the two girls ran so fast, you'd have thought a rattlesnake was after them."

Granny Bert looked at her granddaughter for confirmation. "I thought young people nowadays didn't use paper. They just tap their phones together or hook up through one of those snazzy little apps."

Madison nodded and said with a sigh, "I'm afraid I have to take Miss Wanda's side on this one, Miss Sybil. It sounds like it was a drug deal. Can you describe the girls or the man in the car?"

"All three of them had long hair, that's for sure. And I don't know how one of those girls managed to run in heels that high or in a skirt that tight. She had some sort of streaks in her hair but with all those fiesta lights around the restaurant, it's hard to say what color they were. To be honest," she admitted with a sheepish expression on her face, "I had my hands full with Wanda and wasn't paying them much never mind."

In a charitable voice, Madison assured the older woman, "That's okay, Miss Sybil. I fully understand." They all knew how much Wanda Shanks loved her margaritas, and that she didn't hold her liquor very well.

With a glance at her watch, Madison took a last bite of her streusel. "This is delicious, but I really do need to go. Granny, get in touch with Joyce Williams, please. Also, try to find out who Robby Bishop's girlfriend is. Miss Sybil, if you hear anything else from Dorothy McNutt or about Lula Mae Jones' grandson, please let me know."

She hesitated before bringing up a rather sensitive matter. "There's just one more thing, Miss Sybil. You do realize all of this is confidential, right? This is between us and not... not something you should mention to Otis."

Sybil harrumphed. "Believe me, Bertha has made that perfectly clear!" She slid a cool gaze toward her friend.

Not so long ago, Miss Sybil revealed that she and Otis Perry were seeing one another.

Given that Sybil was her best friend, and Otis her worst nightmare, Granny Bert was having difficulty accepting their relationship. No matter how hard she tried, she just couldn't come to terms with it.

"I simply pointed out that you don't have to tell him everything you do." Granny Bert sniffed in reply. "Not that he's sharp enough to put it all together, but there's no need to dull the blades more than you have to."

"Don't start with me, Bertha," she warned. "Just don't start."

Madison stood from the table. "Okay, you two. Work this out among yourselves. I'm leaving."

She walked away, still shaking her head.

Those two were in their eighties and still squabbling like teenagers.

12

No one ever said stakeouts were glamorous.

While spending the morning staking out *Gilbert's Oil and Lube*, Madison had her own impressions of the job.

Boring.

Tedious.

As exciting as watching paint dry.

Guaranteed to make her sleepy.

Guaranteed to make her hungry.

And, worst of all, none too productive.

Even though Gilbert Herrera and his crew, particularly Jennifer, were the best leads she had so far, the lead hadn't taken her very far.

Shifting in her seat, she added *Bad for circulation* to her list of impressions.

The lube center was located on the highway bypass next to *Gas 'n Go*. Parked in the gas station's parking lot, Madison had a clear view of the vehicles coming and going from *Gilbert's*. She studiously jotted down the make and license number of each one. If she recognized anyone, she added their names to her list.

With Megan home with Brash, it was the perfect opportunity for Madison to get some high-quality snooping in.

Rather, it would be, if anything remotely exciting was happening.

Her plan was to spend the first half of the morning watching the lube center, before heading over to *Myrna's Meadows* to snoop around Timothy Boyle and Lenny George's workplace. She hoped to turn up some useful information there.

Certainly, something more useful than what she found here.

"Ten more minutes," she told herself, "and then you're out of here."

Five minutes later, a man pulled into the lube center in an older-model car. Madison was no expert, but she guessed it could be a car from the 70s. It was two-tone blue, and it was missing its rear license plate.

There was something vaguely familiar about the heavy-set man getting out of the car. Even though a panel van obstructed partial view of the newcomer, she felt like she had seen him recently.

The reasonable thing to do was to leave now and head to the next location. Yet, something nagged at her about the man in the blue car. The more she thought about it, the more convinced she was that she knew the man. She just couldn't figure out how.

Curiosity made her linger. Should she wait the van out, hoping it moved and gave her a better view of the man? Should she get out of her car and find a spot to take a picture of him? Was it even worth it? The man could be anyone.

Brash always said that half the job of good investigative work was having good instincts. He encouraged her to trust her gut. As a mother, he said, she relied on her instincts to keep her children safe and well cared for. It should be no different when dealing with clients and the jobs they hired her for. If something or someone felt off, there was probably a legitimate reason for it.

That instinct kept her rooted in the parking lot of the *Gas 'n Go*. Something told her not to leave yet, and that getting out of her car might not be the wisest choice.

Less than three minutes later, she heard the familiar rumble of motorcycles.

Two men on powerful, shiny machines roared into *Gilbert's* parking lot. Even though Madison had never personally seen the motorcycle gang, she remembered how people described them. Vivid tattoos and leather on their bodies; distinctive flame detailing on their bikes. That was exactly what she saw now as the men did a fancy maneuver with their motorcycles, tires squealing and rubber peeling, before sliding to a dramatic stop.

Their performance drew applause from several of the workers and even a few customers. Apparently, the riders were well acquainted with Gilbert and his crew. Madison could hear their voices from where she sat. They greeted one another with man hugs and first bumps, giving her a chance to zoom in and snap pictures.

Unfortunately, the photos were mostly side views of their faces or the back of someone's head. She needed to be closer, and at a different angle. Just as she opened her door to get out, the men turned and walked toward the building.

Before they disappeared inside, she captured a picture of the insignia on their vests: a four-leaf clover circled by flames identical to the one on their bikes. Inside the clover was the number thirteen.

As she waited for the men to come out, Madison scrolled back through the pictures she had taken. None were suitable enough for facial recognition. The only identifiable things she had were the insignia and the bikes.

The photos did reveal one surprise. Amid the distraction, she had somehow forgotten about the man in the blue car, but there he was on film. That was definitely his back disappearing into the building with the others. That meant her instincts were right. She still didn't know who he was or how she knew him, but he was somehow connected to Gilbert and the bikers. That placed him firmly in her *Suspicious* list.

Several minutes later, the men reappeared, and Madison started her car. When the motorcycles pulled out and took the ramp leading to the heart of town, she followed.

The community known as The Sisters was divided by a railroad track. Naomi lay to the north, and the town of Juliet to the south. They shared a main thoroughfare that branched off into their prospective city streets.

The motorcyclists were careful to avoid the main road stringing the two towns together. Skirting around the downtown areas, they wove their way through residential streets and county roads until they connected with a farm-to-market road. Being the middle of the day, they went largely unnoticed by local residents.

That, Madison surmised, *could be why there were few sightings of the gang.*

Madison drove well behind the motorcycles, yet close enough to keep them in sight. She was surprised to see them turn onto a familiar blacktop road leading out of Naomi. It was the same route she had planned to take for her next snooping excursion.

She had a moment of concern when the motorcycles turned into the flowered entrance at *Myrna's Meadows.* Would they spot her and know she had been following them? Would they confront her and demand to know what she was up to?

She convinced herself that she was overreacting. How else was a person to get from town to the new food truck park? Obviously, she was here for lunch.

Playing it safe, Madison slowed her speed. By the time she pulled in, the men were off their bikes and crunching their way across the far side of the parking lot.

She waited until they were out of sight before opening her door.

The first salad she had gotten from *Toss Up* had been so good, Madison decided to get another. With Megan fixing lunch for Brash once the therapist left, she was free to dine on her own.

"Hey, there," Josie Bargus greeted her with a bright smile. "I see you're back."

"I am. Your salads are delicious."

The owner beamed. "That's what I like to hear! What kind of dressing today?"

"Do you have Italian?"

"Coming right up."

Madison almost felt guilty about questioning the friendly woman, but she had come here to gather information. Josie was her best bet.

"Still liking the new location?" she inquired.

"You know, it's been busier than I expected. I can't complain at all."

"I bet you're glad your friend suggested this place. His name was Larry, right?"

"Lenny," the other woman corrected.

"Is he the one who keeps all this grass cut? Because this is a lot of grass." Madison made a show of looking around.

"Nah. That's his friend Timothy. I feel sorry for the guy, because he may be out of a job soon."

"Really?"

"Yeah. The owner ripped him a new one this morning. Can you believe it was for running over some sort of flower? I heard her screaming at him all the way over here! She claimed it was some sort of special species." With a shrug, Josie added, "It just looked like an ordinary daisy to me."

"That sounds like Myrna, all right," Madison sympathized.

"Timothy's trying to save up money to buy a car, but she threatened to take the loss out of his paycheck. I mean, how much could one little flower cost? I'd think doing the paperwork would be more trouble than it was worth."

"Myrna's flowers are like her babies. There's no telling with her."

"But for cutting down a daisy? The woman's psycho."

"That she is," Madison agreed. "Has she given Lenny trouble, too?"

"Not quite as much. She did make him tear down a bench he spent the whole day working on because she said one leg was shorter than the others. I mean, it was like a hair short." Josie used her fingers to demonstrate. "No one would have noticed, but she made him redo it. She's complained about a few other things, too, but that's the worst of it."

"I hope she doesn't start on you vendors next."

"Me, either. I've just gotten settled and don't want to start all over in a new town." She handed Madison her bag. "Here you go. Anything else?"

"Iced tea, please."

With lunch in hand, Madison found a table that allowed her a wider view of the grounds. She didn't see the bikers sitting nearby. But then her eyes drifted to the *Vape Mobile*, and there they were. The men from the motorcycles and a lanky black man who could only be Lenny. They were laughing and conversing like old friends.

It was another chance at a photo. If she could get their faces, she could send it to Nate, and he could possibly identify them.

Madison pretended to take a selfie of herself and her salad. She posed prettily, but her camera faced forward. She checked the photo—supposedly out of vanity—and readjusted the zoom feature before snapping more pictures. One of the shots showed Lenny passing something to the biker with long, curly hair. Whatever it was, the man slipped it into his pocket without as much as blinking.

The method was so smooth that if she hadn't caught it on camera, Madison might believe she imagined the whole thing.

She needed to take notes while everything was fresh in her mind. She whipped out her notebook and wrote out the latest details. She was still writing when she caught movement from the corner of her eye. The two men from the motorcycles were leaving. As they passed in front of her, she kept her head down, desperately hoping not to call attention to herself.

The men were out of sight by the time Lenny ambled away from the *Vape Mobile* and stopped by Josie's truck.

Under the guise of getting more tea, Madison followed him to the *Toss Up* counter.

Josie handed her the refill, refusing to let her pay for it. "You're just in time to meet that friend I was telling you about," she said. "This is Lenny. Lenny, this is Madison."

Madison turned to him with a friendly smile. "Good job on bringing Josie to town. I can easily get addicted to her salads."

"That's the plan," he replied with a wide smile.

"She tells me you're the maintenance man around here. That must keep you busy!"

"Sure does. Especially with a boss like I have."

"I sympathize with you," Madison assured him. "I know Myrna. I completely understand what you must be going through."

"You should hear the grief she gave my buddy this morning!" Lenny rolled his eyes. "He accidentally cut down one of her flowers, and she went ballistic on him. Threatened all kinds of things."

Madison put just enough worry in her voice to sound sincere. "Josie told me about that. I hope he doesn't lose his job."

"Me, neither. He's using my wheels to get around right now. Sleeping on my couch, too."

"He doesn't live around here?"

"Over in Cougar Springs, but I'm trying to help him out, you know?" Lenny said.

"That's nice of you. Is that where you're from? Cougar Springs?"

"Nah, I've lived all over."

Hoping to encourage him, Madison nodded. "That sounds like Josie. She was telling us the other day that she's originally from California."

"That's me," Josie confessed. "Surfer girl."

"You were living in the desert when I met you," Lenny contradicted. "New Mexico don't have no surfing, girl."

"So? I adapt easily." She shrugged. "Besides, you know the old saying. Have wheels, will travel."

"What about you?" Madison asked Lenny. "Do you just go where life takes you?"

He flashed a big smile. "It's the only way to live!"

"Where has life taken you so far?"

"Let's see... New Mexico, Oklahoma, East Texas,

down by Corpus Christi." He shrugged. "You know. All over."

Madison didn't learn much more after that. She couldn't decide if the relationship between Josie and Lenny was one of romance or simply friendship, but they were clearly comfortable around one another.

On her way back into town, Madison wondered if Josie knew her friend was involved in questionable activity. At the very least, Nate suspected Timothy of dealing drugs, and it sounded as if he used Lenny's car to do it in. That didn't automatically implicate Lenny, but she had seen him with the men on the motorcycles. It may not have been money or drugs they exchanged, but it was something that demanded discretion.

Lost in thought, Madison didn't realize she had company on the blacktop until a vehicle pulled out to go around her. She glanced over and saw a shiny motorcycle in the lane beside her, hovering too close to the center stripe for comfort.

A look in her rearview mirror showed a second bike behind her.

"Okay, no need to panic," she spoke to herself aloud. "We're all traveling the same direction at the same time. I probably slowed down unintentionally, and now, the bikes want around me. No big deal."

Yet, it felt like a big deal. The cyclist beside her was close enough she could see his salacious smile. With no oncoming traffic, he could ride alongside her at a steady rate.

These were the same men from earlier. The Latino with long, curly hair and the stocky Caucasian wearing too many chains.

"So much for going unnoticed," she muttered.

From seemingly nowhere, a third motorcycle appeared behind her.

Madison used the hands-free option on her car to

call Nate. She didn't bother with pleasantries. The moment he answered, she blurted out, "I may have trouble on my hands."

"What's wrong, Mrs. D?" he asked in alarm.

"I just left *Myrna's Meadows,* and I'm being accompanied by three motorcycles. One is riding in the left lane beside me."

She heard the frown in his voice. "That's only a two-lane road."

"Exactly. Are you anywhere near here?"

"I can be." His voice was tight. Within seconds, she heard the wail of his siren over the phone. "I'm on my way."

"There were only two at first. A third one came up from behind. And I think... yes, I see a fourth up ahead!" There was an adjacent county road connecting to the farm-to-market road she traveled, and she could see a motorcycle waiting to pull out in front of her. Nerves made her voice unsteady. "I—I think they're planning to surround me."

"Don't panic, Mrs. D. Keep it steady. Don't speed up, or they'll push you to go faster. Just stay steady. I'm heading your way. Stay on the line while I radio Schimanski and tell him to meet me. Just keep calm."

The fourth rider pulled onto the road as they attempted to block her in. Staying calm was no longer an option.

She remembered something her grandfather had taught her when she first started driving. He told her if she ever found herself in a situation such as this, or if anyone suspicious looking ever tried to stop her on the road, do the unexpected.

Taking her grandfather's long-ago advice, Madison started swerving. She crossed into the left lane, forcing the motorcycle riding beside her to the far edge of the lane. She quickly swerved back again before the bikes tailing her could come up on her right.

Angered by her bravado, the curly-haired biker revved his engine and drove straight toward her. For one terrible second, she thought he might be foolish enough to hit her broadsided. He jerked the handlebars at the last moment and slid his bike in beside her. He was so close, she could see the tattoos on his arms and hands. So close that, if her doors weren't locked, he could reach out and open one.

She kept her eyes on the road ahead, even though she felt his hot gaze on her. Shouting obscenities, he tried to edge her over.

Up ahead, Madison caught a brief glint of sunlight bouncing off a windshield, and she realized they were meeting a car. The man beside her was too intent on harassing her to notice. She deliberately allowed her car to drift his way. It was just enough to feel her side mirror graze against his. Then, with a broad smile on her face, she pointed to the oncoming vehicle.

The man made a classic mistake. Instead of pulling in behind her to be in the correct lane, he pulled left. Crossing the oncoming driver's lane, he had no choice but to head for the ditch.

Madison couldn't look to see what became of him. She had one motorcycle in front of her, two riding her bumper, and she was meeting a car. She had to concentrate on the road.

"Mrs. D, are you still there?"

She realized Nate had been calling her name. "I'm here, Nate," she assured him. "The two bikes behind me are breathing down my neck. I think they may try to ram my bumper."

"If they do, keep both hands on the wheel and keep it steady. Don't let them run you off the road. I'm about a mile away."

"Sadly enough," she told him, "I've been rammed

before."

"Then you should be fine. Just stay steady."

"I am. I'm meeting an oncoming car, so I don't think they'll try anything right now. I see the curve up ahead."

"Great. I'm almost there from this side. Just keep it steady. Slow down like you normally would, but as you get into the curve, I want you to put on your blinker and slow down even more. It should confuse the bikers enough to make them back off."

"If it doesn't, I'll tap my brakes hard enough to make them wish they had."

"Don't try to do anything risky, Mrs. D."

She didn't tell him it was too late for that particular piece of advice.

"I'm coming into the curve. I'm slowing down, but the bikers aren't." A bump on her bumper made her yelp involuntarily. More to herself than to Nate, she muttered, "They wanna play rough? Fine. Two can play that game." She tapped her brakes hard enough to make them bump into her again.

"What are you doing? Don't take any chances!" Nate beseeched. "I'm almost there."

Madison hit her brakes slightly harder this time. One of the motorcycles wavered uncertainly.

"Watch out, Nate. One of them just swerved into your lane."

"I've got eyes on you. Looks like you're doing great. There's a good chance these guys are going to split up and run, so the first chance you get, get out of here."

"Are you sure?"

"I'm sure."

Nothing sounded better.

"Thanks, Nate."

13

Nate was right. The bikers raced off in different directions. One of the bikes behind her made a U-turn in the road and sped off in the direction they had come from. In her review mirror, she saw that the curly-haired man had reappeared on the road and done the same thing. She knew they would split up again, and that Nate would be forced to choose which one to pursue.

Schimanski would face the same issue. The motorcycle in front of her revved its engine and left a trail of smoke in its wake. The one behind her risked gravity and severe road rash as it slid onto its side, managed to come back upright, and made a sharp right turn onto a dirt road. She saw the flash of metal and a trail of blazing dust in her mirror.

She blocked the crazy stunts from her mind and did as Nate told her. Ignoring everything around her, she went straight home and pulled into the safety of their gated entry. There was no denying her nerves were frazzled.

It was a moment before she felt steady enough to walk.

Madison put a smile on her face, but Brash saw

through it as soon as she walked through the door.

"Sweetheart? What's wrong?" he asked in alarm.

"Rough morning." She avoided direct eye contact with him by addressing her stepdaughter. "What have you two been up to? Have you had lunch?"

"I was going to cook while the physical therapist was here," Megan defended herself, "but I looked in the fridge, and there's a ton of leftovers in there!"

Madison managed a smile. "Thanks to your grandma Lydia. She's been like a kitchen fairy, whipping up meals with her magic spoon."

"Madison." Brash's voice was firm. "You're avoiding my question. What's wrong?"

Megan sensed the tension between them. "Do I need to leave?" she offered, half-rising from her seat beside the bed.

With a weary sigh, Madison shook her head. "No. This involves you, too."

"Here, have a seat." Megan offered a chair to her stepmother. The moment she was settled, the young woman said, "Now spill."

Omitting the first of the story, Madison started in the middle. "I drove out to The Grove to get a salad for lunch. While I was there, I, uh, I saw two of the men on the motorcycles."

"Motorcycles? As in... the motorcycle gang?" Given her previous encounter with them, Megan's voice was understandably high.

"I'm afraid so. I waited until they were gone before starting back to town, but a little way out, they reappeared." She glanced at Brash. His face was set like stone. "When a third man joined them, I realized I was in trouble, so I called Nate. He told me to get out of there as fast as I could, so that's exactly what I did. He and Schimanski are handling the men. There's a very good chance Nate will stop by later to take my statement."

"Where is he now? Is he okay?" Megan wanted to know.

"The last I knew, he was in pursuit."

"That's it!" Brash burst out. "I agreed not to have my radio while I was in the hospital, but I'm home now. I want my radio back. I need to know what's happening in my town."

"Brash..."

"I knew all of you were keeping something from me," he thundered. "This is it, isn't it? That motorcycle gang is back in town, and no one bothered to tell me about it!"

"From what I can gather," Madison told him, "there's been a few reports of sightings, but no one's been absolutely positive they were back until now. But it has to be the same ones. They fit the description too well."

"A big black guy with a bald head? A shorter, stockier white guy?" Megan asked. "A Hispanic with long, wavy, black hair, and another dude who's either Hispanic or mixed?"

"I saw the white guy and the one with long hair for sure. One of the men was ahead of me, but I think he may have been black. I never got a good look at the other one behind me, other than when he almost laid his bike over. How he stayed upright, I'll never know."

"Are you just going to ignore me?" Brash demanded. "Didn't you hear me say I want my radio?"

"I did," Madison replied reasonably. "But I don't have your radio. You'll have to take that one up with someone at the station."

"Believe me, I will! Along with a detailed report of everything that's happened since I've been out."

"Sweetheart, you know you're on sick leave. You need to concentrate on your recovery."

"You're telling me four men in a motorcycle gang surrounded my wife, and I'm not supposed to be worried about it?"

"I never said I was surrounded."

"But you were, weren't you? One man was in front of you and at least two were behind you. What about the other one? Behind you or beside you?" he asked pointedly.

She reluctantly admitted, "Beside me." She hastily added, "Until we met an oncoming car, and he had to swerve."

He wasn't mollified. "Maddy, why didn't you call me?"

"Because you're recovering, Brash. Plus, your physical therapist was here."

"It doesn't matter. You should have told me."

"I sort of had my hands full, you know, trying not to be run off the road. I called Nate on the speakerphone, and he stayed on the line with me."

"I want to know exactly what happened."

Madison started over from the middle again, telling him the finer details. She had just finished when Nate texted her, asking if he could come by.

"Hold whatever you were going to say until Nate gets here," she said. "That way, you can chew us both out at once. And no, they didn't catch them."

Megan turned to her father. "Don't you dare chew Nate out! He was helping Mama Maddy. And don't chew her out, either. She was doing what she thought was best for you."

"I'm tired of everyone trying to protect me," Brash complained. "It's not like I'm on my deathbed! What else aren't y'all telling me?"

"I'm just a civilian," Megan claimed, suddenly all innocent. She put her hands up in surrender. "What do I know about police business?"

He wasn't fooled by her meek attitude. "Quite a bit, I'm sure."

Nate arrived soon, and Megan hurried out to greet him. They came in with his arm around her waist, but once he was in front of his superior officer, Nate became all business. "Good to see you, sir." He reached out to shake his hand. "Mrs. D, I'm glad to see you're all right."

"I am, Nate, thanks to you."

"I want a full report, Stone!" Brash barked. He ignored the way his daughter glared at him.

"Yes, sir. But first, sir, I'd like to take your wife's statement. I need to file a report on the incident."

Brash relented somewhat. "You may as well have a seat," he said.

Madison told her story again.

"Can you tell us anything about these men? Did you get a good look at their faces?" Nate asked. So far, they still were unable to ID the men. The first time they were in the area, only a handful of people had seen them up close, and with all that had happened since, the details were fuzzy.

"Just the one with long hair," Madison said. "He was so close to me, I could have stuck my hand out the window and touched him." She shuddered at the thought. "He had tattoos all up his arm and on his hand."

"Anything specific?"

"Flames," she recalled, "like the pattern on their bikes and on their jackets. Several skulls and snakes and evil-looking signs. Don't ask me what, exactly, but they just put off a bad vibe. And I saw the letter M. It was on his arm, and on his knuckles. That, and a 1% sign. Whatever that means."

The two men exchanged knowing looks.

"What? What's it mean?" she asked in alarm.

Brash answered first. "Among bikers, the letter M is usually synonymous with drugs. Sometimes they wear a patch with the number thirteen."

"Why thirteen?" Megan asked.

"M is the thirteenth letter of the alphabet. Back in the day, it stood for marijuana. Nowadays, it usually stands for molly or meth. Either way, it always means trouble," Nate added. "Most people wearing the patch either use or sell drugs."

"I don't remember seeing a patch," Madison murmured. "What's the one percent mean?"

Neither man wanted to explain.

"Tell us!" Megan pressed.

"It's even worse," Brash reluctantly admitted. "A long time ago, the American Motorcycle Association made the statement that 99% of motorcycle riders were law-abiding citizens, and that only 1% didn't fall into that category. After that, outlaw groups called themselves one percenters. It's like a badge of honor for them."

"There's literally a badge," said Nash. "And if you dare wear it, you'd better be big enough and bad enough to prove the claim."

"And these men are here in The Sisters?" Megan was clearly horrified.

Resigned to the truth, her boyfriend nodded. "If not the patch, at least one man wears the tattoo."

"I'll have to get my camera, but I took a picture of the insignia on their jacket," Madison remembered. "That might help."

"Where is it? I'll get it for you," Megan offered.

"Thanks. It's on the bar."

Once she returned, Madison scrolled back through her digital photos and found the clearest one. "Here. Does this mean anything to either of you?"

Nate looked at the photo over her shoulder, but for

Brash to see it, she had to hand the camera to him. "I'd have to run it through one of our databases, but I don't recognize this one offhand," he said after thoughtful perusal. He tried enlarging the picture even more but inadvertently went to the next shot. His brow knitted in a frown. "Where did you take these pictures?" he asked.

"Uhm..." Madison tucked her lips together. "Why do you ask?"

"Because this looks more like an auto shop, not a food truck park."

She tried to take the camera back, but he held it out of her reach. "Maddy. Tell me what's going on."

"It's... I was working a surveillance case for a client," she confessed. It wasn't the full truth, but close enough. "The men just happened to come to *Gilbert's Oil and Lube*, and I followed them out to the food trucks."

Brash narrowed his eyes. "Is that why you suddenly felt a need to have the oil changed in your car?"

"It may have had something to do with it."

"I assumed you were taking it to Rudy's gas station like we always do. I don't like the idea of you hanging around *Gilbert's*."

"Why is that?" She was eager to hear his answer.

"I have my reasons."

"You can do better than that!"

"So can you. What else has been going on around town that you aren't telling me?" He turned his scorching brown gaze to his deputy. The heat was enough to make Nate squirm. "Stone? Is there something I need to know?"

The younger man cleared his throat before answering, "I'd prefer you ask Acting Chief Perry that question, sir."

"I'm asking you."

Nate dared a glance at Madison.

With a dramatic sigh, she said, "We may as well tell him. He's going to pester me until we do. And, frankly, keeping a secret like this is killing me."

"What secret?" Brash ground out.

"Before Nate tells you the official version, I want you to know I was just following doctor's orders. You are in no shape to go into the station yet, and once you hear what Nate has to say, you'll want to be in the thick of it. Just remember that you could do serious damage to your progress, and it's imperative that you stay home." She held up a hand to stop his rebuttal. "I'm not saying don't get involved. I realize that's impossible. But you can do what you need to do from home. Set up a temporary command post, bark out orders on the radio, run background checks and databases... Just do what the doctors and Sid Adair advise. The sooner you heal, the sooner you'll be back at work."

"With a prelude like that," he muttered darkly, "this must be a doozie!" He turned his glare back to his deputy. "Start talking. Tell me what's going on down at the station."

"The quick version? Nothing. Otis Perry is too set on implementing his own ideas to see the crisis we're facing. What's worse, he's tied our hands so that we can't even do our jobs."

"What crisis?"

"Drugs, sir. Drugs have moved into the community at an alarming rate, and Otis simply refuses to see it. He insists the motorcycle gang is the only possible culprit. And while today's incident could reinforce his theory," Nate admitted, "I think it's irresponsible to assume only one source could be responsible."

"Details."

Nate understood the barked command, and he was ready with the answers. After a recap of the egregious crimes, he made an admission.

"It doesn't sit with me, sir, to ignore my oath of office and let these crimes go unchecked. At the same time, I respect the chain of command and know the importance of following orders." He shot a quick glance at Madison and saw her slight nod of approval. "Since Acting Chief Perry has us paralyzed, so to speak, I took matters into my own hands." With a nervous swallow, he admitted, "I hired your wife, sir, to investigate what I can't."

"You did what?"

At that point, Madison butted in. "You heard him. Otis is too full of himself to listen to anyone else. He's started a new urban patrol, for crying out loud! Of course I said I'd help!"

Brash wasn't ready to let the matter go. "I still don't know why—"

Now, Megan was the one to break in. "Yes, Daddy, you do. Think about it. Otis should have never been trusted to fill your shoes. I know the mayor was the one to decide, but he needs to know what damage that man has done in a very short time. He threatened to write officers up for simply doing their jobs. Mama Maddy, on the other hand, can ask all the questions she wants and snoop to her heart's content. Perry can't stop her unless she breaks the law. What other choice did Nate have?"

"He could have come to me!"

"If it makes you feel any better," Madison said, "I was kept completely in the dark until we were home. In just a few days since Nate came to me, I've found out more than Otis has in almost five weeks."

"Why does that not surprise me?" Brash muttered. He rested his head back on the pillow and closed his eyes for just one moment. Madison suspected he was gathering strength for what was to come.

"Okay," he said, "you may as well let me hear it."

"Excuse me, sir," Nate broke in. "Perry's going to be hot when he finds out I left my assigned patrol and responded to a call that didn't come through dispatch. Should I go back to the station and file my report?"

With his signature lift of one brow, Brash's expression meant trouble. In this case, it was for the acting chief. "You leave Perry to me," he assured the younger deputy. "He and I are going to have a talk very soon."

"A talk?" his daughter smirked. "Or a come to Jesus meeting?"

"Whatever it takes," he vowed. "Okay, Maddy. Tell me what you've got."

14

"I have a lot of pieces," Madison began. "I just don't know how they go together. Some are hearsay; some are substantiated."

"Start with the substantiated facts," Brash said.

"Something's not quite right at *Gilbert's Oil and Lube*, and I gather that both of you feel the same. At Nate's suggestion, I did some 'snoopy,' for lack of a better word, on them. I can't say that drugs are involved, but I do know that Gilbert and his girlfriend like to party. What he does in his leisure time is one thing, but I think someone is passing drugs through the lube center. I saw one of his employees, Jennifer, acting very suspicious. After making sure no one was watching, she left a small object at the front of the car. When the customer just happened to walk into the bay, she gave him a discreet nod. That same customer left there and immediately became the subject of Nate's high-speed chase. He flipped the stolen car he was driving and had to be airlifted to a Houston trauma center. No, I can't say for certain they were exchanging drugs, but I can say for certain that it looked suspicious."

Madison moved to her next point.

"I know that Gilbert is well acquainted with members of the motorcycle gang. It could be a personal connection, or it could be business. I saw two of the men there today, and they received a *very* warm welcome. I'm talking man hug, shoulder slap, fist bump kind of warm. Gilbert took them inside a door not generally used by the public and several minutes later, he walked them back out again.

"I followed the motorcycles from there to the RV park, where I saw them at the *Vape Mobile*. They appeared to be friendly with the man behind the counter and with Lenny George, who works for Myrna.

"Lenny is good friends with Timothy Boyle. Timothy is suspected of making at least two drug deals. The one Nate mentioned earlier, and another one that Miss Wanda and Miss Sybil saw outside of *Montelongo's* last week. I also witnessed Lenny pass something to the biker with the long, curly hair, who then slipped it into his pocket. I actually caught the exchange on my cell phone while I was pretending to take a selfie. Again, maybe it's nothing, but it felt like something."

"My head is starting to hurt," Brash muttered.

"Mine is spinning!" Nate said. "Wow, Mrs. D. I'm impressed!"

"Thanks." She flashed him a smile. "Now, for the hearsay."

Brash merely grunted.

"Granny Bert has a theory that the timing for all of this is no coincidence. Aside from the motorcycle gang, the rest of this started after you were hurt, Brash. What if someone is taking advantage of your absence and Otis' incompetency? What better time to start a drug operation here?"

Nate looked thoughtful. "She has a point."

"I suppose," Brash agreed.

"Nate confirmed that several kids at school have gotten in trouble for having drugs. According to certain sources"—they all knew the sources she meant—"Carly McNutt works in the school cafeteria and has recently come into some extra spending money."

She ran down the list on her notepad.

"LaShawn Golden showed up high as a kite at his grandmother's Sunday dinner table.

"Robby Bishop has a new girlfriend who's been around the block a few times, according to his grandmother. He's saving up to buy a motorcycle so he'll fit in with the new rough crowd he's running with. At the moment, he's sitting in the Walker County jail on drug charges.

"There's rumors of strange activity late at night and what people assume are drug deals taking place.

"Town is full of strangers, but very few new people are moving here, per a real estate agent. Again, all unsubstantiated talk, but it has a certain amount of credibility, given everything else we know."

Nate seemed lost. "I don't know any of those people you just mentioned. Who are they?"

"No clue, but those sources certainly know them, plus their entire family history," Madison told him. "The info seems credible."

"He's younger than me, but I knew LaShawn from school," Megan offered. "I can definitely see him doing drugs."

"Okay, so you have lots of pieces," Brash agreed, "but nothing to hold them together."

"I'm working on it," his wife assured him.

"Before we go any further, we need to acknowledge the elephant in the room. What if Otis is right about the motorcycle gang? So far, sweetheart, a lot of what you've mentioned ties back in to the gang."

"Some of it, yes. None of us think they're above

breaking the law, including dealing drugs. But like Nate said, it's irresponsible to assume they're the only ones capable of doing such a thing. We need to keep an open mind."

"Agreed. In view of that, we need to backtrack. I want to see the files on every drug arrest that's been made recently. I want the name of the kids who were expelled from school. I want to know who thought they saw what. If there's a connection between any of the facts and the rumors, I want to know about it."

"Brash..." Madison warned.

"I'm not going down to the station and getting the files myself," he assured her. "I'm going to have Vina bring them to me. I can go over them from right here in this room." He flashed her his most charming smile. "I can even do it while wearing my pajamas."

It's amazing, Madison thought, *what a difference the prospect of getting back to work did for his mood.*

Absolutely amazing.

"Dude, I don't like what's happening."

His friend's dramatic statement wore on Lenny's nerves. "What now?" he asked wearily. There had been a problem with some of the lights around the RV sights, and he had to work overtime. All he wanted was to come in, have a couple of beers, grab a hot shower, and go to bed. He didn't need more of Timothy's high-strung nerves. Especially not the moment he walked through the door.

"The police are watching me," Timothy insisted. "I know they are. They have spies like everywhere."

"Since when do the cops use spies?"

"I dunno. I think it's a small town thing. It was the same way in Cougar Springs. Everyone is watching, everyone is talking. Sometimes, the pigs know what you're going to do before you do!"

"You're overreacting. Chill out, buddy."

"I can't. I know they saw me the other night. I was delivering to those two chicks in front of the Mexican food restaurant, and all of a sudden, the pigs were there. I don't know where they came from, but sirens were going off all over the place. I barely got out of there without getting caught."

Lenny popped the top on a can of beer and handed it to his friend, before getting one of his own. "But you didn't get caught, now did you?" he pointed out.

"No, but I almost did!" his friend insisted.

"Doesn't count," Lenny said smoothly. "As long as you're not sitting in a jail cell, you're okay. Things are good."

Timothy turned the can up and guzzled his beer. "I don't know, man. This is making me nervous."

"I can see that." He did seem overly anxious. "But think about that car. You're earning a nice little nest egg. A few more deliveries, and you'll have enough for a down payment."

"Down payment? I want to buy it outright!"

"Fine. Then buy it outright. It will just take a little longer." Lenny slid a shrewd eye toward his friend. "That, or make more drops," he added.

Timothy didn't answer right away. He stared at Lenny in what he first thought was an angry glare. Then Lenny realized his friend was trying to focus his eyes. And maybe his mind.

"How many more?" Timothy asked, dropping heavily onto the lumpy couch.

"I don't know. Maybe double?"

"No way, man. I barely keep up now."

"Maybe you should work smarter, not harder."

Timothy took offense. "Are you calling me dumb?"

"No. I'm trying to help you double your income."

"Oh, okay." Timothy blinked several times before asking, "How do I do that?"

Lenny eyed his friend in suspicion. "Are you drunk?"

Timothy held up the empty can. "First beer today."

Lenny took him at his word. "Do what I tell you, and you'll double your take. You'll be sitting in that driver's seat before you know it."

"Hell yeah, that's what I'm talking about!" Timothy slapped his knee, but the movement was sloppy. "Just tell me how."

"Tomorrow night," Lenny said, "I'll introduce you to my boss."

"That little round woman who screams all the time? I already know her. She's my boss, too, you know."

"Not that boss, you idiot. *The* boss."

Timothy's eyes had more trouble focusing. His words were sluggish as he stupidly asked, "The singer? Bruce Springfield?"

Not for the first time, Lenny wondered if he had made a mistake bringing Timothy into the business. He wasn't the brightest bulb in the pack, especially when he sampled the product. If he wasn't drunk, he was definitely high.

"His name is Springsteen," he corrected tersely, "and no, I'm not talking about him. I'm talking about the boss of this operation. The man who's paying you to be a delivery man."

"That Bezo guy had surgery?"

"What?" Even Lenny was confused now. "What the hell are you talking about?"

"We work for UPS, right? We deliver packages. And Bezo runs Amazon, right? What happened to him? Why's he having an operation?"

"Dude, you're too messed up for this conversation.

How much weed did you smoke?"

"None." With a goofy smile that revealed stained and crooked teeth, Jeff admitted, "The chick didn't show up for her snacks. I accidentally ripped the package, and the gummies fell out. I didn't want them going to waste."

"And now you're wasted! Those weren't candy, you idiot. They were loaded."

"I tried the fruit punch, too. Nasty-tasting stuff, but I drank the whole thing."

"Go to bed, you moron, before you pass out," Lenny said in disgust. He ran a hand over his head. "Now, I gotta explain to the boss why the money comes up short."

"Bed," Timothy repeated dully. Still fully clothed, he stretched out on the couch. "Hope Bezo's okay." His eyes closed as he mumbled, "I need that car."

15

With Brash in a therapy session and Derron back at his desk, Madison could concentrate on another internet search.

She spent an hour trying to find Jennifer on social media before discovering that *Jennifer* wasn't the only name she went by. Buried somewhere in Gilbert's girlfriend's page, Madison found pictures of the dark-haired woman who also called herself Jazzy.

Judging from the photos, the two women were close friends who had vacationed together in both Vegas and on a sunny beach in the Caribbean. There was no shortage of alcohol in any of the pictures. Madison spotted a bong or two in them, as well. And while the red coveralls had covered Jennifer's tattoos at work, the skimpy bathing suit Jazzy wore in the photos displayed them in their full glory.

Upon closer inspection, Madison realized the tattoo winding its way up her right arm was the same flame pattern used in the bikers' insignia and on their motorcycles. A four-leaf clover covered a spot near her heart.

Did that make Jennifer, aka Jazzy, a member of the gang? Or was it someone she was involved with?

Madison followed the tag to Jazzy Gurl's page. It was filled with images of sport cars, speedway races, and motorcycles. It made sense that she worked in an oil and lube center, working on the very machines she adored.

Jazzy shared post after post of car shows and racing events. Most of her personal posts revolved around motorcycles, men, and parties. Madison ignored the seductive poses and concentrated on what the backgrounds revealed. Most of the parties, it appeared, relied on drugs and alcohol for entertainment.

Strolling further down Jazzy's page, Madison found the proof she was looking for. Jazzy appeared in multiple photographs with the motorcycle gang. There were at least a dozen men on their bikes, with a handful of women draped across their shoulders or lap. Three women had their own motorcycle and their own signature vest. Jennifer/Jazzy was one of the women.

She was definitely a member of the gang.

Clicking through posts and links, Madison finally found a name. The gang went by *Lucky 13*. That explained the four-leaf clover with the same number embroidered inside.

Returning to the top of Jazzy's page, she saw that one man appeared in many of the posts. The highlighted tag identified the man as Grave Robber. Madison clicked on the name and was carried to his page.

"Does no one make their page private anymore?" she wondered aloud. "They don't even try to hide their illicit drug use!"

"What's that, dollface?" Derron asked. "Who's using illicit drugs? None of *my* boyfriends, I hope!"

"Judging from this man's very revealing photos and his disgustingly vulgar posts, I'd say he's definitely into women." She felt dirty simply looking at his page.

She forced herself to stay with it until she found out who Grave Robber's alter ego was. When she saw the name, she cried out in surprise.

"What? Robby Bishop?"

It made sense. Grave Robber and Robby Bishop were the same person, just as Jennifer and Jazzy Gurl were. Robby's grandmother had expressed concern over his new girlfriend and the rough crowd he was now running with. She feared they were having a negative influence on him. Based on what she saw on social media, Madison had to agree.

As much as she hated admitting it, this new information proved one more tie between *Gilbert's* and the Lucky 13's.

Had Otis been right all along? Was the motorcycle gang responsible for the increased drug presence in town?

Needing a distraction from the disturbing thought, she pushed back from her desk and stood. With Brash's session almost over, it was a good time to check on him.

She walked in mid-conversation as Sid was packing his bag to leave.

"Was that when you lived in Athens?" Brash asked.

"Sure was." Sid chuckled. "Actually, I lived there my entire life until I started traveling with this job."

Madison was still amazed at how differently Sid acted in Brash's presence than he did when her husband wasn't in the room. With Brash, the therapist was quite amiable. He laughed and willingly engaged in a two-way conversation. When it was just Madison and him in a room, however, he was borderline rude and sullen. He gave one-word answers when possible. Sometime, he merely offered a grunt. Did he dislike her that much? Or was his affable interaction with Brash part of his duties as a professional caregiver?

Not that it mattered to her. As long as he provided

the best care possible for Brash, it didn't matter how he treated her.

"Do you like that? Traveling, I mean?" Brash asked.

Sid shrugged his shoulders. "It lets me see different areas of the state," he said. "I was down around Corpus for a while, over in the Austin area a couple of different times, up near Granbury, and then around Johnson City. Now, I'm living in College Station and serving this area."

"Sounds like you've just about made the rounds."

"I haven't been out in West Texas yet or up the Panhandle. Maybe I'll apply there next."

Madison knocked so they would know she was there.

"Oh, hey, sweetheart," Brash greeted her. "We're just about done here."

"Don't mind me. I was just checking on you."

"Sid says I can have the weekend off," Brash told her.

Sid conveniently ignored Madison, choosing to address the other man. "You've made remarkable progress so far. I think you deserve a couple of days off. I won't even make you do your upper body exercises this weekend."

Madison offered to walk him to the door, but Sid asked if he could stop by the powder room on his way out. Knowing it would be rude to hover in the hallway, Madison reluctantly agreed when he said he could see himself out.

"I'll start your shower," she told Brash.

"I can probably manage on my own if you have work you need to do."

"He's right about you making great progress, but I still want to be nearby if you need help."

"At least I don't spend the entire afternoon sleeping now. Those first few days were rough," he admitted.

"There's no shame in resting. In fact, it's part of the healing process."

"Maybe so, but I haven't finished looking through all those files Vina brought over. My goal for the afternoon is to get that done before I attempt cross-referencing."

"Just don't overdo it. You know you'll have company over the weekend, so you need to save some of your energy."

"I'll just be reading today and talking tomorrow. Nothing I can't handle."

After a steady influx of visitors the next morning, Madison wondered if he wanted to recant his statement. He would never admit that he was tired, of course, but she encouraged him to rest between callers.

"When my grandpa and uncles get here," Megan informed her stepmother, "Bethani and I are taking you for coffee."

"That's sweet of you girls, but that's not necessary."

"Of course it is," Bethani said. "I know I came home for the weekend to check on Daddy D, but he's going to be in excellent hands with the deCordova crew. It will give us girls a chance to visit while the men do their thing. You know they'll be talking about ranching and sports and all that other manly stuff." The blond-haired young woman waved her hand dismissively.

"Besides," Megan said, "there's a new truck out at The Grove, and I'm dying to try it out."

"I was just here a couple of days ago. I didn't see anything new," Madison contradicted.

"It just opened yesterday. It's called *Coffee and Cream*, and we're going." Judging by the tone of her voice, the subject wasn't up for discussion.

"Yes, ma'am." Madison gave her a playful salute.

Thirty minutes later, they pulled into the entrance of *Myrna's Meadows.*

"Myrna Lewis did *this*?" Bethani asked in disbelief. "I can't stand the woman, but I have to say, I'm impressed."

"I think everyone feels that way," her mother assured her. "She really has done a good job with this."

"Maybe there's hope for her yet."

"I wouldn't go that far. I hear she's giving her employees the blues."

"That figures," Megan said. "I just hope she doesn't drive off her food vendors. Everything I've had here has been really good."

"Same here."

"Well, it's my first time," Bethani said, "so you'll have to show me the ropes."

"This new addition makes four trucks, so that shouldn't be a problem," her sister said.

"Five, if you count the *Vape Mobile*," Madison corrected. "Which I hope you don't."

"Are you serious? They have a mobile vape shop? Are those even legal in Texas?" Bethani asked.

"As long as they don't sell marijuana, and there's no city ordinance saying they can't, then yes." Seeing her daughter's expression, Madison laughed. "I know. I was surprised, too."

"I bet Daddy D just loves this," Bethani murmured.

"There's one good thing about it. If I know Myrna, I imagine she keeps a close watch on them."

There was a nice crowd at the trucks on a Saturday. For the sake of the vendors, Madison was glad.

"The barbecue at *Benji's* is delicious," she advised. "And I can personally vouch for the salads at *Toss Up.* I've had two from there already."

"And even though Granny Bert complains that the

owner isn't a native," Megan giggled, "*Texas Treats 'n Eats* serves amazing fudge."

"I think she's made her peace with the husband. Apparently, he's from Glen Rose," Madison said. "It's the wife she has a problem with." Speaking behind her hand, she confided, "She pronounces it pe-*can*."

Bethani's blue eyes twinkled with feigned alarm. "Oh, the horror!"

"Order any nut but that, or face your great-grandmother's wrath."

"I'm anxious to check out *Coffee and Cream*," said Megan. "It's run by two sisters. One creates the coffee, the other creates the ice cream."

"You and I should have thought of that!" Bethani said.

Long before they became stepsisters, the two started as best friends. Megan was the first friend Bethani made when they moved to The Sisters. The teenager had come here under protest and regularly complained about how corny the town was. Compared to their posh neighborhood in Dallas, the small community was a bit of a cultural shock. Making friends with the friendliest and most popular girl in school had quickly changed her attitude, and soon, Bethani was getting involved in the school and trying out for cheerleader.

Her twin brother Blake had loved it from day one, so it was odd that she was the one to come home most weekends now, when he couldn't. More often than not, his position on the Baylor University baseball team kept him grounded in Waco. His family assured him it was a small price to pay for living his dream, but sometimes, he wondered. As much as he loved baseball, he adored Brash and the country way of life.

"Uh-oh. If Blake sees those two beauties behind the counter, he may forget all about his scholarship,"

Madison predicted. "Shall we go introduce ourselves?"

"Can it wait until after lunch? I'm starving," Megan said.

Madison had eaten with Brash, but she stood in line with the girls while they ordered their food. Both chose barbecue sandwiches and salads.

Next in line to order, Madison overheard someone ask Josie about dressing. She rattled off the choices.

"A friend told me to ask for your special seasoning," the man said.

"Oh, yes. Of course." She reached beneath the counter and pulled out what looked like a one-ounce plastic container. "Will that be all?"

"That's it," the man said.

When she heard the total, Madison wondered what else he had ordered. Perhaps he was paying for several other people, and they had already taken their food. Even ordering every add-on possible, she doubted it would amount to what he paid. He didn't bat an eye, however, as he slid his card into the reader, so she assumed the total was correct.

As they stepped up to the counter, Josie greeted her by name. "Your usual?"

"I've already eaten, but I brought my girls this time."

"How nice! What can I get for you ladies?"

After ordering, they found a table and unpacked their food. "She seemed nice," Bethani said. "And the salad looks yummy."

"It is. But, darn it, I forgot to ask her what the special seasoning is."

Bethani looked down at the colorful garden salad. "I don't see any seasoning on it."

"No, apparently it comes on the side," her mother explained. "The man in front of us ordered it, even though it's not listed on the menu."

"I guess that's what makes it special," Megan said with a grin.

"I guess so."

They visited while the girls ate, and then it was time for dessert.

"Megan says I should try the fudge. Walnut, of course," Bethani added, smiling. "Do you want anything?"

"I'm saving room for the coffee and ice cream."

"Suit yourself. We'll be right back."

Megan's eyes danced behind her stylish glasses. Today, the frames were fuchsia to match the blouse she wore. "Besides. Who said it was either/or?" she teased.

While the girls ordered, Madison observed the crowd. It was a nice mix of young and old, which was best for having a long and prosperous business. Too narrow of demographics could be the death of any venture, particularly small ones like these.

Thinking of her own demographics, Madison stared unseeingly at the people milling about. Should she be worried? Business at *In a Pinch* was slower than normal, but she had been too busy with Brash to really notice. Now that she was back in the office, she noticed her bottom line was thinner than she liked.

There was a man lingering at Josie's counter, but Madison gave him no thought. She was more concerned about whether or not she had allowed her business to slip during her absence.

It wasn't until she heard the man laugh that she did a double-take. She had never heard the sound directed at her, of course, but she often heard it in response to one of Brash's jokes.

Was that *Sid* at the counter? Sid, who lived in College Station and said he was off this weekend? He made a point to tell Brash they would both be enjoying a relaxing weekend. According to him, he saw patients two weekends a month, but this wasn't one of them. What was he doing back here in The Sisters?

Her eyes trailed him as he left the food truck. The girls were just returning, so she asked them if they would excuse her. Without explanation, she took the path Sid had taken. Instead of turning toward the parking lot, he had turned in the opposite direction. Madison decided the path led somewhere other than to the RV park.

She still had eyes on him as he passed through the trailer entrance. Maybe he was seeing a patient, after all. Maybe they lived here at the RV park.

"But where's his bag?" she murmured. She hung back, making certain he didn't see her.

Hiding behind an ornamental shrub, Madison watched the medical professional stroll leisurely through the park's main road. There were a few more filled spots than before, but there was ample room for more. As he walked toward the furthest row, she noticed he carried no food bag in his hand. Either he hadn't ordered, or she hadn't noticed him eating at one of the other tables.

Turning into a pad occupied by a top-of-the-line, towable RV, he glanced over his shoulder. Madison shrank behind the flowering shrub, hoping he didn't see her there. There was already enough of a strain between them; finding her spying on him would only make the tension worse.

The trailer door faced her direction, giving her a clear view. Without knocking, Sid opened the door and went inside. She waited for a few minutes, but he didn't come back out.

Did that make this *his* RV? And if so, why did he tell Brash he lived in College Station? Surely, he wasn't embarrassed about living in an RV, particularly in one this nice! He traveled for a living, so taking his home with him from place to place made more sense than renting an apartment, and it was certainly more cost effective than staying in a hotel. If Madison ever found herself in a similar situation, she thought she might make the same choice.

As Madison stepped away from the shrub, she heard voices nearby. She looked up to see Lenny and Timothy coming up the same path Sid had just taken.

"I told you, man," Lenny said. "You gotta sober up before tonight. I can't take you with me if you still look like this!"

"I ain't drunk. And I wasn't drunk last night."

"No, you were high."

"I don't know what that chick ordered, but I've never had nothing like that before," Timothy insisted. "What kind of gummies were those?"

"I told you. They were CBD, laced with something extra."

"And the punch?"

"That wasn't punch, you idiot! It was cough medicine. The kind with hydrocodone in it. And you were stupid enough to mix it with loaded gummies and beer. It's no wonder you passed out last night and are just now waking up," he groused.

The men were coming closer, and Madison didn't want them knowing she had overheard their conversation. She dashed behind the fence that separated the RV park from the rest of the complex.

Once they passed through the entrance, however, they would see her there. Hearing their footsteps on the gravel road, she knew she was running out of time. There was a delivery truck parked behind the food trailers, but it was too far away. Even if she ran, she wouldn't make it in time to use it as camouflage. The men were closing in fast.

Turning her back to them, Madison leaned over at

the waist and pretended to be sick.

Seeing her, Lenny tentatively offered his help. "Hey, lady. Are you okay?"

Keeping her face averted, Madison waved them away. She made a gagging sound and bent deep.

"Gross!" she heard Timothy exclaim.

"Yeah, let's give her some peace," Lenny suggested. The sound of their hurried footsteps soon faded.

Madison waited before rejoining the girls at the table. "Sorry I took so long."

"Is everything all right, Mom?" Bethani asked, concerned.

"Oh, yeah, sure," she answered vaguely. "I just saw someone I knew."

The girls accepted her excuse at face value. "We're done with our dessert," Megan said, "and are ready for coffee. What about you?"

Madison smiled. "Coffee sounds great."

Mindi and Mia Robertson owned the newest addition to The Grove. *Coffee and Cream* combined their favorite things and funded their online college courses. Mindi, the sister with the shoulder-length hair the shade of honey, was studying business. Mia, with her short, sandy-colored hair, was a liberal arts major.

"Are you from around here?" Megan wanted to know.

"We moved to Riverton almost two years ago. We don't really look like it, but we're twins," Mia explained.

"You are? Sweet! I'm a twin, too," Bethani said with a broad smile.

Mindi waved a finger between her and Megan with a question in her eyes.

"No, I have a twin brother. His name is Blake. Megan is my stepsister."

"Ah, that explains the difference in coloring. Blond hair and blue eyes, versus green eyes and auburn hair."

"Blake has blond hair and blue eyes, too. And if I do say so myself, he's the most handsome boy you've ever seen," Madison put in. "The next time he's home, I'll send him by."

"Where is he?" Mia asked.

"He plays baseball at Baylor. They like him to stay close to campus, but that will change after the season is over."

She scrunched her face in confusion. "It's baseball season? I thought that was in the summer."

"As you can see," Mindi laughed, "my sister isn't much into sports."

"Fair enough. But I meant that after the spring season is over, Blake will be classified as a junior, and the rules are different for juniors and seniors."

"If he's as cute as your mom says," Mindi quipped, "that might be good to know!"

"Would a mother lie?" Madison asked innocently.

"Oh, no, never."

"What's the best coffee you make?" Bethani asked.

"All of it, naturally," Mia answered.

For good measure, her twin added, "Just ask yourself. Would the owner of such a fine establishment lie?" Her expression mimicked the one Madison had worn.

After paying for their coffees, they looked for another place to sit and enjoy them.

"I like them, don't you?" Megan said.

"I'm definitely bringing my brother here the next time he comes home," Bethani agreed. "Mia isn't into sports, but I think Mindi would make a perfect match for him."

"All these *M*'s could get confusing, though," her stepsister worried. "Mama Maddy, Megan, and now Mindi. We may have to give her a nickname."

"Girls!" Madison laughed. "You just met her ten

minutes ago! Don't be marrying her off to your brother just yet. He should at least meet her first."

"Good idea." Bethani grinned. "Meet, then marry."

"More *M*'s," Megan noted.

As the girls giggled at the joke, Madison's mind wandered. She recently learned that *M* could stand for many things.

Marijuana. Meth. Molly. (She looked it up and discovered it was slang for ecstasy.)

The list was ongoing. Magic mushrooms. Motorcycles. Misery.

Nate had said it best. When it came to gangs, the letter *M* meant nothing but trouble.

16

The moment Madison walked into the room, she could see that Brash was exhausted.

"The company was nice," he admitted once they were alone, "but it's been a full day. Is anyone scheduled to come?"

"Just the sandman," she answered as she rearranged his pillows. "I think you need to call it a day and get some rest."

"I hate to say it, but I think you're right. As much as I enjoyed seeing my brothers, all their stories and jokes wore me out."

"If someone happens to drop in, I'll ask them to come back tomorrow."

His protest was weak. "You don't have to do that."

"I think I do. You can barely keep those gorgeous brown eyes of yours open." Madison leaned over to kiss him. "Now, go to sleep, my love. Call me if you need me."

The only drop-in visitor they had was her grandmother. Madison didn't feel at all guilty about telling her the truth.

"I was just going to say hi anyway. It was you I really came to see," Granny Bert admitted.

"Do you want to sit in the breakfast nook or somewhere more comfortable?"

"You know how I feel about kitchen tables. Mine has seen many a meal and many a precious memory." It wasn't often her grandmother became sentimental, but her scarred kitchen table got her every time. She had fed her husband and their four boys around it. As her family grew, her grandchildren gathered around it, and then her great-grandchildren. Problems were solved at that table. Dreams were spun, and sorrows eased. The dining room table was reserved for company and big gatherings, but family and close friends always gathered in the kitchen.

It was the same way here at the Big House. The old mansion had a formal dining room with its fancy furniture and famous hand-painted mural, but most meals and conversations took place here in the breakfast nook.

"What's up?" Madison asked once they were settled.

"I found out a little more news I wanted to share."

"Great. I need all the information I can get, because right now, we're all stumped. Even with Brash's help, there's something I'm missing." With a frustrated huff, Madison admitted, "As much as it pains me to say this, right now, most of the signs point to the Lucky 13's."

"Who in tarnation are the Lucky 13's?"

"I found out that's the name the motorcycle gang goes by. And yes, as much as we all hoped they were just an avid club, they are definitely a gang. They have the patches and tattoos to mark them as the worst of the worst."

"One percenters, huh?"

"How do you know that?" she asked with a gasp.

"I was the justice of the peace for years, girl," the old woman reminded her. "Don't think I didn't learn a thing or two during all that time. I even had my own motorcycle after your grandfather died, and I ran up against a few unsavory characters, you know."

"No, I didn't know." Madison's tone was indignant. "You had no business riding a motorcycle at that age. And you certainly had no business mixing with people like that!"

"You only live once, and you may as well make it count. When I leave this earth, I'm leaving with no *I wish I had*s hanging over me."

"Yeah, well, you're leaving your family with frayed nerves," Madison muttered thickly.

"Are you going to complain all evening about my life adventures, or do you want to hear my news?"

Justly reprimanded, Madison gave in. "I want to hear your news."

"Joyce Williams has been keeping an eye on Carly. She's noticed how Carly talks to certain kids more than she does others, and how they all seem to ask for a straw, even though she doesn't handle the drinks. More than once, she says Carly reached under the counter and handed them an extra straw."

"I guess that could explain how she passes the drugs to them, but how do they pay her?" Madison wondered.

"I don't know, but Joyce noticed Carly has been wearing new clothes lately, and they're not the brands you get at *Walmart*."

"Good to know. Tell her to keep up the good work."

"Oh, she's happy to give us the lowdown on Carly. The two of them don't get along, so she's hoping she can get enough dirt on the girl to get her fired."

"If she's selling drugs to these high school kids—or to anyone, for that matter—she needs to be fired."

"I have more news. I was talking to Benji's mother yesterday. I asked how his business was going and if he liked it out there. He said that other than dealing with Myrna and some of the other vendors, he's pleased with how things are going."

"I get the Myrna thing, but what about the other vendors?"

"According to Joan, that little gal with all the rabbit food doesn't get along with the guy from the *Vape Mobile*. They're always arguing about something."

Madison was surprised to hear it. "Josie? Her salads are delicious, by the way, and not rabbit food. And she seems so likable."

"Not by Chris, she's not. He's the guy who owns the vape truck. Joan said Benji is getting fed up with listening to them fight."

"Hmm. I've never ventured down to his trailer, so I don't know a thing about him."

"Well, get this. The guy moved his business here from Stockton Bend."

Madison stared at her blankly. "Is that supposed to mean something? I have no clue where that is."

"It's in Hood County, a good couple of hundred miles up the Brazos River from here. Just outside of Grandbury and only a half hour from Glen Rose."

She still didn't understand. "And?"

"And that little pe-can girl and her husband came here from Glen Rose. Don't you think it's odd that two of the four food trailers out there come from the same area?"

"Maybe a little," Madison conceded. "But there's five trailers now. The girls and I went there this afternoon. It's run by two sisters about my girls' age, and they make great coffee. If you want something cold, they also have all sorts of ice cream shakes and sundaes."

"The more the merrier, I always say. But what are the odds of two trucks coming to a tiny little town like The Sisters from the same area? It seems suspicious to me."

"Are you sure this doesn't stem from the way the *Texas Eats 'n Treats* lady butchers the name of our state tree?" Madison teased.

"The pecan isn't just our state tree. It's the official state nut and the official state pie. Anyone who lives here should at least know how to say it! *Puh-kaan.* Native Americans gave it that name, and we should honor it!" Granny Bert tapped the table for emphasis.

"Okay, don't get worked up about it. I agree with you. I think her name is Louisa, and yes, she should know how to say the word correctly. But maybe the fact that she and her husband are from the same area as the vape shop guy is just a coincidence. Or maybe they're friends, like Josie and Lenny. Maybe one of them talked the other into coming here."

"Who's Lenny?"

"The maintenance man for *Myrna's Meadows.* Apparently, he and Josie have been friends for a while. He got the job here and suggested she bring her food trailer and set up shop."

When Granny Bert twisted her lips, a swarm of wrinkles followed. "And none of that sounds odd to you?"

"The fact that one friend wants at least one familiar face in a new place? Not really."

"Where did the salad girl come from?"

"Austin."

"You're telling me she leaves the state capital with its two million plus potential customers and moves to a little town with only three *thousand* people in it? Why would she do that?"

"Less competition?" Madison suggested. "Less congestion? She said something about going where the wind blows her. She's originally from California, by way of New Mexico."

"Still doesn't make sense that she'd come here, of all

places. Not unless she's in love with this Lenny fella."

"I don't think that's it. I think they're just friends."

"So, you're saying the maintenance man has a connection to one of the food vendors, and that two of the other three vendors—now four—also have a connection? And you don't find that odd?"

"Now that you say it like that..."

"I think we should look into this food truck thing. Maybe these people run in packs, but it just seems awfully coincidental to me. Plus, they all showed up at one time."

Madison looked thoughtful. "But even so, where's the harm in that? Myrna must have advertised, and one friend told another. There's nothing illegal about that."

"Maybe." Her grandmother sounded doubtful. "I know that vaping has become a common thing now, and that vape shop owners deserve a shot at free enterprise the same way everyone else does. As long as it's legal," her grandmother qualified. "But that's the thing. A lot of those shops aren't legal, and it's an easy way to sell weed. In the Lone Star State, only CBD oil is legal."

"You think that's what the *Vape Mobile* is doing? Selling weed?"

Granny Bert lifted her shoulder. "I hear they have a questionable clientele."

The image of Lenny and the biker came to mind, and whatever they passed between them. And there was no denying Lenny had close ties to Timothy Boyle. She didn't know if Timothy was a dealer, but he was definitely a user. 'Loaded' CBD gummies, prescription cough syrup, and beer? Depending on the quantity and strength he took, he was lucky to wake up at all.

"And it's not just that," her grandmother continued. "Arlene and her sister-in-law made peace long enough to have lunch out at the food trucks. Jolene noticed the tattoos on both owners of *Texas Eats 'n Treats*. Marijuana leaves, plain as day." Another tap on the table suggested it was proof of her claim.

Madison disagreed. "That doesn't mean the *Vape Mobile* deals weed. These people may not even know each other, even though they come from the same area."

"All the same, Wanda and I are going out there."

"Are you sure Miss Wanda is the best choice?" she asked dubiously.

"Sybil was willing to gather information, but I'm afraid that's where she'll draw the line. As much as it pains me to say it, I'm just not sure I can trust her when it comes to Otis. Gathering intel is one thing. Proving he's a blind moron is another."

Madison nibbled her bottom lip. She didn't comment on the 'intel' statement, as if their gossiping was a matter of national importance. Among Granny Bert's network, it probably was.

After a long pause, she shared her worries with her grandmother. "What if he's not? I mean, yes, he's a moron. But what if Otis is right on this one? What if the motorcycle gang is behind all this? I saw one of the members at the *Vape Mobile*, and it looked like he and this Chris guy were well acquainted. It was the same with Lenny. I'd say they're all friends."

"I refuse to believe Otis Perry could be right about anything," Granny Bert huffed. "This just means we have all the more reason to check out the *Vape Mobile*, and Wanda Shanks is the perfect person to do it."

Madison practically whined. "But it's Miss Wanda. As much as I love her, she can be unpredictable."

"Leave everything to me, girl," Granny said confidently. "I've got this."

The food park was closed on Mondays, but Granny Bert and her friend visited on Tuesday.

"Ooh, it all smells and looks delicious!" Wanda rubbed her hands together in anticipation. "I'll have to bring Derron out here. I know he'd love it!"

Derron rented her spare bedroom, and the two had become like family. They shared the same childlike spontaneity and an appreciation for all things fun. As frustrating as their impulsive whims and quirky ways could be, they were both oddly endearing.

"Remember," Granny Bert said, "we're here for a purpose."

"Absolutely." When Wanda vigorously nodded her too-black hair, her double chins wobbled, and her entire body shimmied. "To eat lunch and snoop. Two of my very favorite things."

Their first stop was *Benji's Barbecue.*

"Why, look who it is!" He smiled. "Two of my favorite ladies in The Sisters! How's life treating you two these days?"

Granny Bert's "I'm fine" collided with Wanda's list of complaints. "My car's been acting up again, so I guess I need to get it checked out. I had a bout with my gall bladder, and now, Lucky Ducky seems to be ailing. I do hope it wasn't contagious."

"Lucky Ducky?" the man asked.

"My support duck," she explained, as if it was the most common thing in the world. "I should have brought him with me. He would enjoy the outing, especially if there's a pond. I'll bring him the next time I come."

Unsure of how to respond, Benji asked what he could get for them.

Wanda was quick to respond. "I'll have the two-meat plate. Link sausage and brisket."

"That sounds good," Granny Bert decided. "But just brisket for me."

"Coming right up."

When he handed them their food, Granny Bert stepped closer to the counter. "Your mother tells me you've had some trouble with some of your neighbors."

Benji slid his eyes toward the *Toss Up* truck. "I reckon you could say that."

She didn't pretend not to know the details. "At least their trucks are separated."

"Yeah, but he's always down here. Even if she goes to him, you can still hear their voices. They fight like cats and dogs. Always arguing."

"Can you tell what they're arguing about?"

"Not really. I try to tune them out, but sometimes, it's impossible."

Settling at a table, Granny Bert asked Wanda if she wanted a salad.

"Bad for the gall bladder," she claimed.

"And you think sausage and barbecue isn't?"

Wanda just shrugged. "It's worth the risk."

Between eating and listening to Wanda chatter, Granny Bert observed their surroundings. There weren't many people at the food park today, but maybe that was to their advantage. The new *Coffee and Cream* trailer was the busiest of all.

Granny Bert noticed one woman buying a coffee and taking it with her to the vape truck. After a brief conversation with the man who was presumably Chris, he pointed her in the direction she had come. She retraced her steps and stopped at *Toss Up*.

The two vendors may have their issues, Granny Bert thought, but at least Chris had sent some business Josie's way.

Seeing the way her companion watched their exchange, Wanda commented, "I like that woman's hair. How do you think I'd look with pink and blue streaks in mine?"

"Ridiculous."

Wanda took no offense at the blunt reply. She shoveled another bite of potato salad into her mouth.

The customer apparently ordered a small salad, judging from the size of the container. She must have asked for something else because Granny Bert saw Josie's eyes dart about before reaching under the counter and slide the item her way.

Something about the exchange brought to mind what Joyce said about Carly. The cafeteria worker would slide an extra straw toward certain kids when she thought no one was looking. Josie had done the same thing now, except with a plastic container rather than a plastic straw.

It was certainly worth noting.

"Are we getting ice cream next, or fried Oreos?" Wanda wanted to know.

"I'm still eating my barbecue."

"I wanted to save room for dessert." In consideration of that fact, Wanda had left a few morsels on her plate. A slice or two of onion, three pickles, half a piece of bread, and a sliver of brisket. "But I think I'll get a refill of tea."

When she returned, it was with more than just tea. She had an assortment of fried treats, plus a square of fudge.

"You went without me?" Granny Bert asked.

"Don't worry. I plan to share," Wanda assured her.

"I didn't so much want the food as I did the information."

"What would you like to know? Louisa and I chatted while Danny fried up a fresh batch of treats, just for us."

"First-name basis, are you?"

"You know how quickly I make friends. Anyhoo, they moved here from Glen Rose, where all those dinosaur tracks were found. They used to make a funnel cake in the shape of the footprints." Easily sidetracked, Wanda said, "By the way, did you know that the Apatosaurus had hind feet that measured three feet in length? They didn't make their cakes that big, though. Just a miniature version."

"That's a relief."

Her sarcasm was lost on Wanda. "Can you imagine the size of box they would need for a three-foot funnel cake? And how a person would carry it? It's best they stuck with the smaller version. They first started making dinosaur track-shaped treats when they were out in New Mexico. Louisa said they had a three-toed version that was super cute. Of course, out there, their business wasn't called *Texas Eats 'n Treats*. They called it *Dinosaur Highway Eats 'n Treats*, since that was the area they were in. And before that, they were *Desert Eats 'n Treats*."

"Let me guess. They were in the Arizona desert."

"Exactly! She says she doesn't know where they'll go next, but they'll keep the same concept, and the same Eats 'n Treats suffix."

"That's all they do? Move from place to place?"

"Yep. No kids to tie them down, so they just go where the business is."

Granny Bert narrowed her eyes. "And The Sisters, Texas seemed to be the most logical place."

"If you ask me," Wanda said, lowering her voice, "I think it was a bad business decision. I don't think they'll be here long, but while they're here, I'll enjoy their food. These fried cookies are really good!" She popped another into her mouth. "Help yourself."

"Thanks, but I'm not a fan. I'll probably get ice

cream on our way back from the vape shop." She put a wrinkly hand on her friend's puffy arm. "Now, remember, Wanda. We're only buying, not smoking. Got it?"

"I should at least try it, to see if it's flavored tobacco or something more."

"It's that *something more* I'm worried about. Weed isn't the only thing that can be used for vaping. It can be the hard stuff, too, like LSD." She put pressure on Wanda's arm. "No vaping," she repeated sternly.

"In that case," her friend huffed, "let's just get this over with!"

17

As the two elderly women approached the *Vape Mobile*, the proprietor smiled with amusement.

"Well, well, well, ladies. What can I do for you?"

"Are you Chris?" Wanda asked.

"Sure am."

"Good. A friend said you could fix me up."

His smile faded. "A friend, huh? What friend?"

Wanda looked around, as if checking for anyone who might overhear their conversation. "We don't use names," she said. "Plausible deniability and all that."

Amusement once again flickered in his eyes. "Now, what does a sweet little old lady such as yourself know about plausible deniability?"

"Who are you calling old?" she demanded.

"Who are you calling sweet?" Granny Bert echoed.

"Now, now," Chris said, backing away slightly. "Don't get upset. I meant no insult. Let's start over. Are you looking for something specific? A flavored tobacco, perhaps? Vanilla is always a popular choice."

Wanda rested a fist on her full hip. She was wearing a blue blouse with large white polka dots on it. She touched her too-black hair, its blunt cut best suited for women a fourth her age. "Do I look like the vanilla type to you?"

Chris chuckled. "I can't say that you do. Something spicy, then, like cinnamon?"

"Something spicier than that." She leaned closer and said in a loud whisper, "My friend said you had the good stuff."

"The, uh, the good stuff?" he stalled.

Granny Bert pretended to panic. "Whatever you do, mister," she implored him, "do *not* sell her the good stuff! You should have seen her down in Mexico. She almost started a cartel war. She can't be trusted with anything stronger than nicotine."

"Oh, poo! Don't listen to her, Chris. She's just jealous because Carlos... oh, we don't really need to get into that, now do we? I'm just looking for something to entertain me, and my friend said you were the man to see. But if he was wrong..." Wanda shrugged, leaving her words dangling.

Chris took the bait.

"He's not," he assured her quickly. "I'm sure I can accommodate you ladies."

Granny Bert grunted. Loudly. "No ladies to it!" she complained. "It's just my friend, and she don't qualify as a lady. I want nothing to do with this tomfoolery. I'm just here to drive the getaway car, so to speak."

Five minutes later, Wanda walked away with a smirk and a little brown package.

"Easy peasy," she said. "That man had 'sucker' written all over him."

"Remember, you are *not* sampling!" Granny Bert hissed.

Wanda cut her eyes toward her with a sly look. "You know, the doctor said I could use medicinal marijuana."

"That doctor wasn't in Texas, so, no, you can't. We're taking this to Nate. He'll take it from there."

"Not if Otis finds out."

"You're right. We'll give it to Vina," Granny Bert decided. "Even Otis is smart enough not to mess with Vina."

"Or we could just give it to Brash."

"Who would have to give it to Vina, since he's stuck at the house. No need bothering him with this. We'll save him the effort and take it to Vina ourselves. Here, let me carry that."

Wanda handed the package over with reluctance.

"You won't let me vape, so can we at least get ice cream?" she whined.

"I swear, Wanda Shanks, sometimes you sound just like a child!"

"I take that as a compliment. Young at heart, young in spirit."

Granny Bert harrumphed. "Wrinkled in reality is more like it."

"Which is why I try to keep my wrinkles plumped out the best I can," Wanda informed her smartly. She stepped up to the counter of *Coffee and Cream.*

"Ladies," she said with her widest smile, "show me your menu!"

Granny Bert took full credit for the mission.

"My plan worked like a dream," she said later that afternoon. After taking the package directly to Vina, she stopped to give Madison her full 'report.' Genny's presence made the victory that much sweeter.

"You mean Miss Wanda pulled it off?" Madison asked. She put a hand to her chest in relief. "I was worried about that."

"It was actually a little scary," Granny Bert confided, "hearing that woman rattle on about the particulars of certain drugs the way she did. Sometimes, I can't help but wonder about her."

"I don't know about that. Wanda Shanks strikes me as someone who can hold her own!" Genny laughed.

"I think you're right. And the important thing is, we took the e-cannisters and turned them over to Vina. She'll know what to do with them."

"Otis will be furious when he finds out you went behind his back to do this," Madison warned.

Granny Bert smiled broadly. "That's the best part!"

After giving the situation serious consideration, Brash had chosen not to reprimand his senior deputy.

Yet.

An official rebuke was coming, but for now, Otis was still the acting chief of police.

Brash concluded there was no reason to tip their hand concerning the drug activity. If the perpetrators believed their deeds had gone undetected— or, better yet, had been blamed on someone else—they would be more likely to make a careless mistake. Nate hadn't been happy about the decision, but he trusted in Brash's wisdom and respected his choices. For now, they would proceed as if nothing had changed.

The truth, however, was that everything had changed. Nate, Madison, and Vina were all working behind the scenes—and behind Otis' back—to gather incriminating evidence. Most importantly, Brash was involved now. The drug dealers didn't know it, but their days in The Sisters were numbered.

As usual when Madison was involved, her grandmother and her friends found a way to be involved, as well. Madison still worried there could be a backlash from today's 'mission.'

"You didn't have any problems?" she asked again. "You didn't see anyone from the motorcycle gang, right?"

"Nope. The only issue we had was when we were leaving," Granny Bert reported. "We were almost sideswiped by a delivery truck. Genny, do you use *Jim's Restaurant Wholesale?*"

The blonde shook her head. "I've never even heard of them."

"Apparently, they supply the food trucks," Madison said. "I saw a truck out there on Saturday."

"On a Saturday? Wow. I'm impressed. I don't know of any suppliers who run on the weekends."

Madison shrugged. "This one must, because I saw them out there."

"Well, someone needs to teach them how to drive," Granny Bert complained. "The guy came this close to knocking my mirror off." Madison suspected the measurement may have been off, but she didn't call her on it.

"I'll have to look them up. Jim's, you said?" Genny asked.

"Yep. *Jim's Restaurant Wholesale.* The logo wasn't very big, but I could read it easy enough. Oh, and speaking of looking things up. Maddy, you really need to look into this *Texas Treats 'n Eats.*"

"Why? Did the vape guy say something?"

"No, but Wanda struck up a conversation with them, and I'll be, if she didn't dig up more dirt than I did! They went by the same name in Glen Rose, where they made funnel cakes in the shape of dinosaur prints."

"Hey, I went there one time when I was a kid!" Genny said. "Dinosaur Valley State Park. There were fossils and dinosaur tracks in the river bed and huge life-size renditions of what scientists believe they must have looked like."

"Wanda says it's a good thing they didn't make the cakes true to size, which was about three feet long. She was worried about the box they would have to come in." Granny Bert shook her head in amusement. "Luckily for Louisa and Danny House, they had previous experience with smaller dinosaur tracks out in New Mexico. There, they were called *Dinosaur Highway Treats 'n Eats*. Before that, they were *Desert Treats 'n Eats* out in Arizona."

"Not only do they have a 'fry everything in sight' mentality, but they show the same lack of imagination in naming their businesses," Genny noted.

In turn, Madison's brow puckered. "They certainly move around a lot, don't they?"

"They plan to keep the same concept and the same name, minus the location, when they move again next time."

"Did they say why they live like nomads?"

"Some malarkey about going where the business takes them. Even Wanda could see through that flimsy excuse. There's not enough business here in The Sisters to attract flies! And certainly not out at the RV park."

"If they've lived in all of those places," Madison said thoughtfully, "they must have left a trail."

"What do you want to bet that the trail is littered with drug charges?" Granny Bert speculated.

"Granny," she chastised. "Just because they move around a lot, and just because they have marijuana leaf tattoos everywhere, doesn't automatically mean they have a criminal past."

"But they have a connection to Chris, and he's a criminal. He knowingly sold drugs to Wanda and me today. Plus, he's set up in the same park as they are. That's proof enough for me."

"Supposed connection," Madison pointed out. "We don't know yet if they were simply from the same general area and if they knew this Chris before they moved here."

"Mark my words. There's a connection," her grandmother insisted. "In fact, I think all three of those trucks are in cahoots, plus that maintenance man. I haven't even told you about your friend Josie yet."

"What about Josie?"

"Benji confirmed that she and Chris are constantly arguing. He doesn't know what it's about, but he says they can get pretty loud. So, I thought it was strange when I saw a customer go up to the *Vape Mobile,* and Chris pointed her back down to *Toss Up.*"

"Maybe she got the two of them confused."

"A vape shop and a salad truck? Seriously?"

"Okay. Then, maybe the woman asked Chris where she could get a salad, and he was nice enough to suggest Josie's."

"I could understand that," Granny Bert allowed. "But that doesn't explain what happened next."

"Which was?"

"The woman ordered a small box of something, and then she appeared to ask for something else. Josie looked around like she was making sure no one saw her, and then she took a little plastic container from beneath the counter and slid it to the woman, all smooth-like."

"Was it like one of the those black, one-ounce containers with a lid? The kind used for bacon bits and such?"

Granny Bert nodded. "It looked about that size."

"Saturday, I overheard a customer order something called special seasoning, and she took it from beneath the counter. It's not on the menu, and I forgot to ask her about it. That must have been it."

"Maybe. But it reminded me of what Joyce Williams said about Carly."

"Carly McNutt?" Genny asked. "What has she done now?"

"The same thing as Josie. She makes sure no one is watching before she slides an extra straw over to certain kids. She does it all smooth-like, too."

Madison bit her lower lip. "What are you saying, Granny?"

Genny answered for her. "I think she's saying your friend Josie could be dealing drugs. I know that everyone certainly suspects Carly McNutt is."

The thought of Josie dealing drugs was upsetting. Madison truly liked the woman with the colorfully streaked hair.

Later, when she looked up the name Josie Bargus, very little came up. She eventually put in Josephine Vargus, and the page filled with hits. The images that popped up showed a woman with dark hair, but the features were the same. Along with her hair color, her would-be friend had obviously changed her name.

Probably to hide her checkered past, Madison acknowledged. The list wasn't too egregious, but it put a new spin on her opinion of the woman.

The House couple had a past similar to Josie's. Like her, most of their offenses were minor. Speculation of impropriety and questionable activity plagued them all.

The Houses had, however, been under scrutiny for tax evasion and ignoring zoning laws. As with their menu and their trade name, when they found a winning formula, they stuck with it; the same suspicions and the same scrutiny followed them to each location.

Had they chosen The Grove because there were no zoning laws?

And how had she missed the fact that they, too, had lived in New Mexico? It seemed too coincidental that Josie, Louisa and Danny House, and Lenny had all lived in the same state, at the same time, and that they now all lived in The Sisters. She didn't know Chris' last name and nothing came up for the *Vape Mobile*, but if she could look him up, would she find that Chris, too, had lived in the other state? Instincts told her that she would.

There was one silver lining to her discovery. From what she could find, the Lucky 13's had no ties to New Mexico. Neither Gilbert, his girlfriend Terri, nor his employee Jennifer/Jazzi had ties to The Land of Enchantment. That meant that if the drug deals were connected in some way that didn't involve the motorcycle gang, Otis Perry had been wrong all along.

At least in some small way, a semblance of order had been restored to Madison's world.

18

The next morning, another envelope addressed to *Grayson, McGarvey, and Associates* arrived. Inside was another purchase order, with the same confusing descriptions.

Yet today, the descriptions didn't sound quite as confusing. Madison couldn't quite put her finger on why, but something about them made more sense now. The quantities still struck her as strange, but she felt a glimmer of hope. Some sixth sense told her she was on the verge of a breakthrough.

She carried the envelope with her when she checked on Brash.

"How's your session going?" she asked. She looked around the room. "Where's Sid?"

"He just left."

"He did? I didn't hear the chime on the door."

"Guess you just missed it. But the session went well. He says that by the weekend, I should be able to put enough pressure on my leg to use a cane, instead of a crutch."

"That's wonderful, sweetheart! I know you can hardly wait."

"It's been a long time coming, that's for sure," he

said.

"Ready for a shower?"

"Sid suggested I take a hot bath, instead, as long as I stay off my leg."

"I think that's doable. I'll go start your bath water."

"Thanks, babe."

"Oh. When I get back, can I look at that letter I left with you? The one with the crazy purchase order?"

"I looked for it the other day. I thought you had it."

"No, I'm sure I left it here with you. You were going to look up some stuff on the computer."

"Which I started, but then I couldn't find the envelope."

"Well, you're in luck, because I received another one." She held it up for him to see.

"Did you get one last week?" Brash asked.

"You know, I don't think I did. With everything that happened, I didn't even notice."

"Mind if I look at that one while you start the bath water?"

"Of course not." She handed it to him. "I'll be back in a jiffy."

There was a frown on her husband's face when she returned.

"Hey. You're much too handsome to be wearing that look. Is something wrong?"

"I don't know yet. Maybe."

"What? Is it something about the letter?"

"Yeah," he admitted slowly. "Let me think about it while I'm in the tub."

"Okay, but the idea of a tub is to let you relax. Can you do that, thinking about whatever is making you frown?"

"I sometimes have my most brilliant ideas while relaxing," he told her.

"That's doubtful, but whatever. Come on. I'll help

you into the tub. You can come to your brilliant conclusion, and then you can share it with me."

"Sounds like a plan."

It was another thirty minutes before the topic came back up.

She had helped him from the tub, at which point he stubbornly insisted on dressing himself. He even sat in a chair while they ate lunch. The show of independence had taken its toll and he was now back in bed.

"So. Did you have an epiphany?" Madison asked with a smile.

"No, but I do have a theory."

"You do? Let's hear it."

"The thought has been rolling around in my head since the first time you showed me that purchase order. And given what I now know about recent activity in town, my theory feels more plausible than ever."

"I *knew* there was something going through your mind when I showed that to you! What it is? What have you figured out?"

"There are still several things I don't understand. The quantities, for instance, and the unit sizes. Most of all, I don't understand why these are addressed to your late husband's defunct company, and why they're coming here. Especially after all this time."

"The same things have me stumped," she murmured. "But oddly enough, I feel like I know what the descriptions are. I just can't quite put my finger on them."

"I think I can help you with that."

"Please do," she said eagerly.

Brash ran a long, lean finger down the order form. "See this description for MultiMix? It's designated as either red or blue."

"Yes, I saw that. Is this for a candy store? An assortment of blue candies and an assortment of red?"

"I think you've got the assortment right, but it's far from being candy. Barbiturates often have street names that include the word red. Reds, red devils, red birds. You get the picture. Drugs like fentanyl, oxycodone, and methamphetamine are sometime called blues. Blue, blues kisses, blue diamond, blue dolphin."

Madison paled when she heard his explanation. "Brash, that's scary."

"You're right. And this one. Straws. I think that refers to blow, or cocaine."

She gasped. "Carly McNutt has been slipping extra straws to kids at school! She serves food, not drinks, but when someone asks for an extra straw, she pulls them out from under the counter. Brash, this is terrible!"

"I'll call the superintendent this afternoon. We need to shut this down."

"What are all those other things? Like Tumblers?"

"Could be rock cocaine. And two ounces is a common weight to sell."

"A two-ounce tumbler," she whispered.

"I'm not sure about the Pouches or the Special. Candy could mean marijuana gummies."

Biting her lip, Madison nodded. "I think I know what some of it means. I overheard Timothy Boyle tell his friend Lenny that he drank some punch, but what he really had was prescription cough syrup. And he had gummies that Lenny said were 'loaded.'"

"That makes sense. And the special could stand for special K, or Ketamine. Or any special mix of any drug." His sigh was heavy. "It's hard to say."

With a sinking feeling in her stomach, Madison admitted, "Whatever it is, I—I think I know who's selling it. Remember I told you about Josie, the woman who runs the *Toss Up* truck? Well, on Saturday, I heard someone ask her for some special seasoning, and she pulled out a little one-ounce container to give them." She blew out a breath. "It's not on the menu board."

Brash looked thoughtful. "We know—or think we know—that drugs are being sold on campus and at this *Toss Up* place. Where else?"

"*Gilbert's,* for sure. That Jennifer/ Jazz person is hardly a Girl Scout." A thought occurred to her. "What if those numbers in the quantity column are code for different dealers? I always wondered why they were so low, and why everything wasn't written together. Maybe one is the school, two is *Gilbert's,* and so on."

"Good idea. Unfortunately, these numbers go all the way up to seven. That means at least seven dealers."

"Uh-oh. You have that look on your face. The one you get when you want to tell me something, but you aren't sure how to say it."

One corner of his mouth lifted in a smile. "You're right," he said, yet he offered nothing more.

"Well?" she cried in exasperation. "Aren't you going to tell me?"

"There's been a new trend lately, called a sweep. A crime organization targets a particular town or community, and their dealers sweep in. Their job is to recruit and set up multiple drop points. If one location gets shut down, there's always two more to back it up. Once they have their drop points and new pushers in place, they move on to the next place and do it all over again."

"That's horrible. And you think they've targeted The Sisters?"

"Makes sense. There's a new food truck park in town. A couple of new businesses. I think Gilbert came in first to test the market, and now someone above him is doing a sweep."

Madison couldn't help but gasp. "You think Myrna is involved? I mean, I don't like the woman, and she organized that campaign to get you ousted from office when we first got married. But I didn't think she would ever stoop *this* low!"

"I'm going to give her the benefit of the doubt. She almost went bankrupt when she bought up all that land, thinking she could make a quick dollar by selling it back to a developer. Then the deal fell through, and she was stuck with empty buildings and land she can't afford. Now, she's put a small fortune into her RV park. Where do you think she got the money?"

"I have no idea, but you're right. It must have cost a fortune. Just wait until you see it."

"I think someone came to her with a proposition and offered to bankroll a new venture. She probably saw it as a way to pay off her debt and make a little extra."

"So, you don't think she's part of the organization?" Given her opinion of the woman, Madison was oddly relieved.

"No. I think it's probable she's a victim of her own greed."

After a long moment of silence, Madison spoke.

"Back to this sweep thing. I have to agree with you. Granny Bert insists there's a connection between the owners of *Texas Eats 'n Treats* and the guy who runs the *Vape Mobile*. They all moved here from the Glen Rose - Grandbury area, and she thinks it's no coincidence. Plus, I've discovered some other connections, too.

"Lenny, the maintenance man at *Myrna's Meadows*, brought Josie to town and befriended Timothy, a down-and-out slacker who is suspected of dealing drugs. Lenny and Josie first met in New Mexico, where Louisa and Danny House once lived. They're the ones who own *Texas Treats*. All of them have a string of petty charges that stretches from one town to another. It makes sense that they're part of this sweep mess. Josie claims she goes wherever the wind blows her, but I think it's more like she goes where the big boss sends her."

"Get me their names and information, and I'll run them through our criminal database. It's much more thorough than a simple internet search, or you snooping through their social media pages." Brash threw her a knowing look, until he saw the expression on her face. "Uh-oh. Now you have that look. What don't you want to tell me?"

"Well, uh, something else happened yesterday that you aren't going to be happy about."

Brash's voice sounded more resigned than angry. "What is it?"

"Granny Bert and Miss Wanda—"

He put his hand up in protest. "Whatever it is, I already don't like it."

"Keep in mind, they were only trying to help. They did a little snooping of their own, and they wound up at the *Vape Mobile,* where Miss Wanda... well, she sort of bought some illegal drugs from the guy."

"She *WHAT*?" Brash yelled.

"We don't know for sure that they're illegal," she was quick to say. "Vina is having them tested."

"And you didn't think to tell *me* about this?" he thundered.

"We thought we could get the report back and then tell you."

His face was as dark as a thunder cloud. "You're telling me that Wanda Shanks deliberately bought illegal drugs. That's a criminal offense, you know."

Realizing her error, Madison backtracked. "Uhm, did I say that? Because I meant to say she bought some canisters from him, and there's a possibility they *could* contain illegal drugs."

"Madison." His voice was hard.

"Brash," she returned.

"This isn't funny!"

"I know it's not. And believe me, I'm not laughing. But they were only trying to help. No one, even your officers, can stand the thought that Otis might be right about the motorcycle gang. This new information doesn't rule them out as the masterminds, but it gives us another possibility, right? It sheds new light on the case."

"But it's your grandmother and her group of geriatric troublemakers!"

"In all fairness, Miss Virgie and Miss Sybil are innocent. This is all Granny and Wanda Shanks."

"If that's supposed to make me feel better, it doesn't. It's bad enough that you're involved in this," he growled. "The last thing we need is those two 'helping!'"

Brash was right about the sweep.

The men had perfected their method long before it had a name. Long before it became a trend among other organizations.

Their strategy had always been to keep one step ahead of the law. Like a rolling stone, they didn't stay in one place long enough to gather moss. Or unwanted attention, as the case may be. They got in, set up their operation, and got out. After countless towns and multiple states, their business ran like a well-oiled machine.

In their business, there was never a lack of customers.

"I think it's all coming together now," the older man said.

"Did you have any doubt?"

"Not really. I've done this so many times, I could do it in my sleep."

"Still worried about some of those newbies?" his companion asked.

"A couple. One is too brazen for his own good. It landed him in jail for a few nights. The other is too skittish. And I think he may have helped himself to some of the goods. He came up short last week."

"You know what to do with slackers. And most definitely with cheaters." The younger man held his fingers in the shape of a gun. As he took aim, he smacked his lips together and made a loud *pop!*

His partner gave a loud sigh. "Do you ever get tired of it?"

"Of the money? Never!"

"There's more to life than just money, you know."

"Name one thing," the man challenged, his voice ungiving.

"Peace."

"Peace? We can have all the peace we want once we're dead. While we're living, we can have wealth. And power. Exactly what we have now."

"I'm getting older. The truth is, I'm thinking of retiring. I'd like to spend my golden years in peace."

"Why not spend your golden years in gold?"

The older man slowly shook his head. "One day, you'll understand."

"Well, that day ain't today. We're in this for the long haul. And you know the old saying."

"What's that?"

"'Till death do us part."

19

"We may have a problem." It was the first thing her grandmother said when the phone rang.

Madison braced herself. "What kind of problem?"

"A Wanda Shanks kind of problem."

"Oh, Lord. What has she done now?"

"Come down here, and I'll explain."

"Where are you?"

"Oma and Opa's."

"I can't. Brash called Superintendent Reeves, and I'm waiting for him to get here. Why don't you just drop by here, instead?"

"Well, that's the thing. Wanda sort of hijacked my car," Granny Bert admitted.

"What? Why would she do that?"

"I'll tell you about it while we're out looking for her. She'd better not hurt my car!"

"I told you I'm waiting for—Oh, I think I hear him at the front door."

"Great. I'll see you in a few minutes." Granny Bert hung up before she could reply.

"So much for sitting in on their discussion," Madison muttered to herself. "Instead, I have to go look for Miss Wanda, the car hijacker. I don't know which one Granny is more concerned about: her friend or her car." She started toward the front foyer to greet the school superintendent. "If Brash learns about this, I'll never hear the end of it."

Madison assumed her grandmother would be impatiently waiting for her on the sidewalk, but she was clearly wrong. Disgruntled, Madison had to go inside to retrieve her.

She found her at a back table, talking with an unfamiliar man. When she reached them, Granny Bert made the introductions. "Madison, this is Harvey Mulkey. He's putting in a pet store in the old *Boundaries* building. Harvey, this is my granddaughter Madison deCordova."

"A pet store?" Shaking his hand, she tried to keep the surprise from her voice. Why would someone put a pet store, of all things, in their little towns?

Then it hit her. The sweep. Myrna owned her late sister's old building, after buying it from Derron. Given the nature of business, she felt certain it was part of the scheme to bring drugs into town. No one would be surprised when the pet store folded and closed up shop.

Barely listening to the conversation, Madison thought about the new businesses that had come to town in the past year. *Gilbert's Oil and Lube* and the food trucks at Myrna's, of course, plus a new thrift shop called *Second Chances*. Two new beauty consultants who sold products online and out of their homes. This very café where she sat.

Was everyone suspect? It was a crazy thought, but at this point, nothing seemed too outrageous to consider.

The moment the man said his goodbyes, Granny Bert grabbed her handbag. She waved Emma Klein away when she approached the table with a smile and a coffee carafe. "Nothing more for me, Emma. Madison just came to pick me up."

"Yes, I noticed your friend made a hasty exit. Is she okay?" Her face puckered in concern.

"I'm not sure. We're going to check on her."

Emma looked at Madison. "I'm sorry, but I couldn't help but overhear your grandmother introduce you. Your last name is deCordova? I don't believe I knew that."

"Yes, that's right."

"Any relation to the chief of police? I understand he's injured and on sick leave at the moment."

"I'm happy to report that he's on the mend and growing stronger every day. And yes, you might say we're related by marriage. He's my husband," she said with a proud smile.

"Oh. Oh, I didn't realize that." She looked truly surprised. "Well, I'm glad to hear he's doing better. And I won't keep you two ladies. I know you're concerned about your friend."

Once outside, Granny Bert cocked her head to one side and said, "Something strange is going on."

"Yes, but it is Miss Wanda we're talking about." Madison unlocked her car with the key fob. "Hop in, and you can tell me why she took your car, and how we're going to find her."

"One thing at a time," her grandmother said as she hoisted herself into the seat. "I'm talking about what Emma just said."

Madison fastened her seatbelt. "What was that?"

"She claimed she was a big fan of *Home Again*, yet she didn't know you were married to Brash. Don't you find that strange?"

"Maybe. I mean, we weren't even engaged when we wrapped up filming. I guess it's possible she didn't think we were that serious."

Granny Bert rolled her eyes. "Please! It was obvious

you two were head over heels in love. Marriage was inevitable!"

Madison had to agree. Their relationship had played out on national television, which was part of what made the show so widely popular.

"Speaking of husbands..." Madison said. "Have you ever seen hers?"

"Once. I went to the ladies room, and he was in their office, barking out orders to someone on the phone. His German temper was on full display!" She chuckled. "And of course, there's that framed article about them at the register. Your cousin Dane ran the story when they opened."

A thought tickled in her mind, but Madison didn't take time to dwell on it. They had more important matters at hand.

"Okay, where are we headed, and why did Miss Wanda hijack your car?"

"Well, she and I got to talking about the case over lunch, and we—"

Madison interrupted her. "About that. I think it's best that you lay off for right now. This could be more serious than we first thought."

"Are you kidding? We have a new theory, and it's worth checking out. In fact, I suspect that's what Wanda is doing."

"Alone?" Madison cried. "We have to stop her! Where is she?"

"That's what I don't know, and what you're going to help me figure out."

Madison backed out of the parking space. "I'll start driving, and you start looking. And talking! What's this new theory of yours?"

"We got to thinking about that delivery truck that nearly ran us over. That Jim's wholesale company that Genny's never heard of. The one who delivers on

Saturdays, when no one else does. I tried to look them up online, and there's no mention of them."

"Nothing?"

"Nothing."

"Maybe they're new, or maybe they just don't have an online presence."

"Or maybe they're fake."

Madison took her eyes off the road to look at her grandmother. "What?"

"Think about it. No one's ever heard of them. They drive one of those generic white vans, with a vinyl logo on their side. I remember that it was wrinkled in one place, meaning it wasn't painted on."

"That doesn't mean they're not legit."

"No, but it would be a smart concept, wouldn't it? No one would think twice about seeing a delivery truck unloading their products. But what if that product was illegal drugs?"

"Okay, so it's possible," Madison admitted. "And sort of diabolically brilliant. Do you have any proof?"

"We're working on that. We saw the van at *Gilbert's* and thought it looked suspicious."

"Why? They were probably getting their oil changed."

"They weren't in one of the bays. They were backed up to the far side of the building. Why would a restaurant supply place be at an oil and lube center?"

"Maybe they stock the lunchroom for their employees. And I know they serve coffee there. It tastes terrible, but they have to buy it and the cups somewhere."

"No matter. Seeing it there was what got us to thinking. You have to admit, it makes sense. They go to all the places we suspect of selling drugs. Maybe not to the school, but to *Gilbert's* and the food trucks."

"That still doesn't explain why Miss Wanda ran off

in your car and left you stranded."

"She forgot her purse in the car, so I gave her my keys to unlock the door. She had just come back in, the keys still in her hand, when she saw the delivery van driving down the street. Before I knew it, she jumped in the car and took off after it."

"Okay, there's no need to panic." She said the words to herself, as much as she did to her grandmother. "We're going to find her. Let's check the food trucks. Maybe they went out there."

Halfway there, Granny Bert said, "I know I'm prone to drive a little fast, but the way you're driving is sure to get you a ticket."

"I doubt it. Otis probably pulled everyone off traffic duty to chase down some serial litterbug."

"Sad, but true."

Madison bumped over the landscaping timbers leading into *Myrna's Meadows*. She may have plowed down a plant or two as she took the corner too fast. "Myrna is going to kill me for that!"

"We'll deal with her later," Granny Bert said. "Look! There's my car! And it looks to be in one piece."

"What about Miss Wanda? Do you see her anywhere?"

"She probably went around behind the food trailers, looking for the delivery truck."

Madison parked beside her grandmother's car and threw open her door. "I'll run back there and look. This *is* Miss Wanda we're talking about."

"Good idea. You go on. I'll catch up to you."

Madison started to slam the door, but she ducked her head inside to issue a warning. "I hate to do this to you, but here comes Myrna, and it looks like she's on the warpath. Can you deal with her while I go look for Miss Wanda?"

"I'm spoiling for a fight right about now," Granny

Bert assured her. "Leave Myrna to me."

Madison took off at a sprint.

"Madison deCordova, you stop this minute!" Myrna Lewis screeched in her abrasive voice. "You just ran over my flowers, and that's destruction of property. I demand that you pay for the damages."

Madison ignored the woman marching her way. Huffing and puffing, Myrna crunched over the gravel drive in her crew socks and orange tennis shoes. With no fashion sense whatsoever, she wore blue shorts and a psychedelic t-shirt with mostly pink and yellow swirls. Her customary fanny pack was fastened somewhere near her nondescript waist.

"Not now, Myrna," Madison called as she ran past her. There wasn't time to pacify the irate woman. "But Granny Bert is in the car. Take it up with her."

She heard Myrna bellowing behind her, but Madison didn't slow down until she reached the food trucks. A small lane ran behind them, tucked up against the RV park's wooden fence. It was just wide enough for essential vehicles to travel.

The *Jim's Restaurant Wholesale* van was parked behind the Houses' bus. Almost hidden behind the rear tire on the far side, Madison spied a familiar pair of orthopedic shoes.

Making certain the coast was clear, Madison slipped around the front of the van to reach her. "Miss Wanda," she hissed, "what are you doing?"

"What do you think?" she hissed back. "I'm spying on them."

Madison crowded around her. "What are you going to do when they move the van?" She kept her voice in a whisper.

"I don't know yet. He's still inside the bus."

"Maybe we can go that way, around *Coffee and Cream*," Madison suggested.

"I don't know. I think I hear voices now. They must be coming out."

When she started to peek around the back, Madison stopped her with a hand on her arm. "They'll see you."

Miss Wanda shook her head. "He can't see the back from where he is, and he's already closed these doors. We're good." She took a few tentative steps forward and peered around the other side. Just as quickly, she plastered herself against the back of the truck.

Madison edged toward her. "What's happening?" she whispered.

"The owners are outside, and he's getting in the cab."

Thinking fast, Madison unlatched the hasp and shoved on the handle of the roll-up door. It moved a grand total of about two feet. Its rattle was masked as the truck's engine rumbled to life.

"Get in," she told the older woman.

"I can't!" Miss Wanda hissed.

"Get in or get caught."

It was almost comical watching Miss Wanda's attempt to crawl into the truck. She couldn't get her leg up high enough to make the threshold. She finally laid over on her side, and Madison rolled her in, using her shoulder for extra *oomph*. As the truck started to roll forward, Madison dove inside and managed to pull the door down. It wouldn't latch from the inside, so she was forced to keep pressure on the handle until they were away from the lane.

It was a temporary solution. There was a stop sign ahead. When the drivers stopped before pulling onto the highway, the stowaways would crawl out.

Unfortunately for them, the driver didn't heed the sign. Seeing no oncoming traffic, he accelerated to make the turn.

"Madison!" Miss Wanda cried. "Now what?"

"Shh. The driver may hear us." Being a typical delivery van, the box in the back wasn't completely separate from the cab. A narrow pass-through distinguished their different spaces. "Stay toward the sides of the truck."

"I'll try, but I keep rolling!" Like a child, she thought it was funny.

"Stop laughing!" Madison hissed. "He'll hear you."

"He'll see you," she shot back. "Why are you back there?"

"Trying to hold the door down."

"You can't hold it the entire way!"

Madison didn't point out they had no idea where they were going, or how far away it was. Two other issues took precedence. "If the door comes up, it may suck us out," she whispered. "Or he'll stop to close it and find us in here."

"We're in trouble, aren't we?" She heard the warble in Miss Wanda's voice.

"Maybe not. Text Granny Bert. Tell her to follow this van!"

Madison's arms were already aching. She was lying flat against the floor, stretched out to keep as low of a profile as possible, while still holding the door handle. She knew her muscles would give way before long.

"Start inching toward the front," she told Miss Wanda. "Crawl if you have to, or roll. Don't let him see you, but get as close to the front as you can. I can't hold these doors much longer."

She managed to keep her position until Miss Wanda was nearly to the front. When she could no longer hold on, Madison turned loose of the handle and scooted away as fast as she could. After several bumps and a few potholes, the door inched upward. It jingled with every bump and groaned at everyone pothole.

The driver glanced into the rear-view mirror and

saw the gap of daylight. "Not again!" he wailed. "I thought I latched that!"

He kept driving, glancing back every so often. Madison silently begged Miss Wanda to stay where she was and not move.

A phone rang, and her heart sank. Would the sound give them away? It wasn't her ringtone, so it must have been Miss Wanda's.

When the driver answered on the second ring, relief washed over her. "Hello. Yeah, I'm almost back to town." He listened to what the caller had to say before replying. "Fine. I'll meet you in my office."

Madison didn't recognize his voice.

At last, she felt the van make a sharp turn, and the driver killed the engine. She stayed in place while the man got out of the cab and walked around to the back of the truck. Madison noted as many details as she could before he pulled the door down and latched it in place. She knew they were parked outside, in what seemed to be a parking lot. She saw the side of a red pickup and what looked like a two-toned blue classic Chevy.

The car from Gilbert's!

The last thing she noticed before the door came down was the man's rounded belly and brown pants held up by suspenders. Then the door rattled shut, the hasp clicked in place, and the van was quiet.

And dark. While her eyes adjusted to the dim light, Madison whispered, "Miss Wanda?"

There was no answer. "Miss Wanda?" she asked a little louder.

Still nothing. Growing worried, Madison groped around until she felt the older woman's arm. Giving it a shake, she spoke still louder. "Miss Wanda!"

"Wha—What?" When she finally answered, she was clearly startled.

"Were you *asleep*?" Madison asked incredulously.

"I closed my eyes to say a prayer, and then I guess I fell asleep. Was I snoring?"

"Who could tell with all that road noise?"

"Are we still moving?"

"No. We're stopped. He locked the back, so I'm going to crawl through the front and see where we are. If the coast is clear, we'll get out. Did Granny Bert answer your text?"

"I'll look." She fished inside her pants pocket to find her phone. "Oops," she said sheepishly. "I forgot to press send."

Madison didn't reply. She crawled through the opening, over the console, and into the driver's seat. They were at the back of some building. She thought it looked vaguely familiar, but didn't most alleyways look the same?

"I don't see anyone. I think you can come out now."

Miss Wanda pushed slowly off the floor, a small groan escaping her lips. But the groan turned to a giggle when she had trouble squeezing through the gap between the cab and the back of the van. By the time she turned and tugged and eventually tumbled across the console, she was laughing.

"Oh, my, what a story to tell the girls!" she said. "And Derron! He'll wish he had been here with us." She laughed some more as she attempted to clear the smudges from her blouse and succeeded only in smearing them. "What a sight I must be." She looked at Madison and started laughing all over again. "You! You should see yourself! You're filthy."

"I don't care. I'm calling Brash."

He answered after the first ring.

"Brash, I'm not sure where I am, but Miss Wanda and I may be in trouble. We hitched a ride in the *Jim's* delivery truck—I'll explain later—and now, we're in a parking lot somewhere."

"You what? Hold on." She could tell he switched the call to hands-free. "I'm looking on Family Circle. It looks like you're behind the *Fresh Starts* building."

"*Oma and Opa's*? Are you sure?"

"If they're in Myrna's building where *Fresh Starts* used to be, then yes."

Completely surprised, she was slow to answer. "Okay. Uhm, I guess ask Nate to meet us here. No lights and sirens. I'm not sure what's going on yet."

"Are you okay?"

"Filthy, apparently, from lying on the floor of the truck, but yes. So far, we're both fine."

"So far?" he asked in alarm.

"It's a long story, but yes." She put an unsteady hand to her forehead, more shaken from their ordeal than she realized. "Look, I need to figure out what's going on. Just call Nate for me. I have to call Granny Bert. Love you."

"Be careful!" he instructed in a stern voice. His tone softened as he said, "I love you, too, sweetheart."

As she hung up, Miss Wanda reported, "I sent the text to Bertha. She answered and said she knows where we are. She's on her way."

"How does she know... oh, that's right. Family Circle." Once again, the app to keep track of their family's whereabouts had proved itself useful.

"Are we going to sit here all day, or can we go in? I need to find a little girl's room."

"Apparently, we're sitting behind *Oma and Opa's*." Madison looked at her phone to confirm their location.

Miss Wanda looked relieved. "Oh, good. They won't mind if I use theirs. Come on. That's the back door right there."

Getting out of the truck, Madison scanned the parking lot. The two-toned Chevy seemed to mock her.

She had seen the car at Gilbert's. Something about the heavy-set driver had seemed familiar, but she hadn't been able to place him.

Granny Bert's words from earlier drifted into her mind. *"...there's that framed article about them at the register. Your cousin Dane ran the story when they opened..."*

Madison's hand came up to her chest, where her heart had surely stalled.

She was at the back of *Oma and Opa's.* The building was one of Myrna's.

The man in the two-toned car... the man in the article... the man driving this very truck. She realized they were the same person: Leon Klein. One half of *Oma and Opa's.*

Emma hadn't been fan-girling that day when Granny Bert and Miss Virgie were giving their 'reports.' She wasn't starstruck; she was eavesdropping! Like Granny Bert pointed out, the woman hadn't even watched *Home Again.* Quite likely, someone had told her it offered a plausible excuse for coming to The Sisters.

The truth stared Madison in the face.

The Kleins, that sweet little German couple who made such delicious streusel, were as dirty as Madison's clothes.

What's more, they were involved in the sweep!

20

"Are you coming?" Wanda asked. She was already halfway up the steps to the restaurant's back door.

"I don't think that's a good idea," Madison told her.

"I don't think tinkling on the sidewalk is a good idea, either. You can stay out here if you want, but I'm going in."

Madison hurried up the stairs behind her. "Not without me, you're not!"

With her arm muscles still weak, Madison had to wrestle the door open. The hallway lighting was dim. Coming in from the bright sunshine, it seemed particularly dark.

"I can't see where I'm going!" Wanda giggled, bumping into one of the walls.

"There," Madison pointed. "That door says '*Frauleins.*'"

"I guess that's us!" She pushed the door open but stopped short. "Oops. One-holer."

"That's fine," Madison assured her. "I'll wait out here in the hall."

Madison dusted at her clothes while standing there, but a strange noise caught her attention. It sounded like gurgling. Was it coming from the kitchen? Maybe it was a rapidly boiling pot.

Or was that someone wheezing?

She cocked her head to one side, trying to determine where the noise came from. Was it back here, or was it coming from the dining room? What if someone were choking on their food?

Madison started toward the front, until she heard it again. Another painfully slow intake of air. Ragged, like someone was in distress. This time, she thought it came from the room on the right.

With a perfunctory knock, Madison pushed on the door. Typical of old buildings, the wood scraped against the jamb. It stuck for just a moment, but a final push did the job. The door opened.

Boxes were stacked everywhere. She assumed she was in a storeroom until she saw the desk, strewn with papers. A chair was pushed away from it, still wobbling from recent movement. Had someone gotten up quickly? Had they gone in search of the noise, just as she was doing?

The sound came again.

Was that from behind the desk? More curious than she was alarmed, Madison skirted a stack of boxes to reach the other side.

She stifled a scream when she saw him. The man from the delivery truck. The one with the rounded belly and the pants with suspenders. The one who was part of the sweep.

Leon Klein lay in a heap on the floor. His stared at her as if begging for help, but all he could manage was one last ragged breath.

After that, the room grew silent.

Madison knew that any effort to save him would be in vain. The man was already dead. She knew that, even before noticing the knife in his back.

Madison slowly backed out of the office. She knew

she should call for help. She knew she should call 9-1-1. She should call Nate. But her head was still reeling from her recent revelation that Leon Klein was part of the sweep.

And now, Leon Klein was dead.

Numb with shock, all she could do was back her way into the hall.

"Hello, Madison."

She heard someone say her name. The voice was low and solemn, and oddly familiar.

She swung around to see who was behind her, surprised to come face to face with Sid Adair.

It was the closest she had ever been to the man. He was always so cool and aloof toward her. He never got too close. He never spoke first. In fact, he spoke to her as little as possible, even to the point of being rude.

Why did he wait until *now* to be friendly? Now, of all times, when she had just stumbled upon another dead body!

She tried to speak, but the words stuck in her throat. *Was* he being friendly? Something in his eyes gave off the opposite impression. And something in his eyes suddenly seemed very familiar...

"Has it really taken you so long to recognize me?" he asked in reproach. "You've seen me almost every day for three weeks, and you still don't know who I am?"

"S-S-Sid?" She had trouble pushing the name out.

"Try again."

Madison looked closer, focusing on his eyes. Hers widened when she made the connection.

"McGarvey?" she gasped. "McGarvey Orr?"

He was bald now, but at one time, he had dark, wavy hair. That was back when he was young and thin. It was no wonder she hadn't recognized him.

"That's right, Madison. It's me. Your old buddy from way back."

Madison wanted to tell him that they had never been buddies. That she never understood how Gray and he could have been friends, much less partners. The man was greedy, pompous, and self-centered. He used people, including his wives, for what they could do for him. He cared about no one but himself.

He had never been her buddy.

"Why—Why do you go by the name Sid Adair now?"

"That's a long story, and I'm afraid we don't have time for that now."

The fog slowly lifted from her brain. "You're right. I have to call Brash. Or 9-1-1. I just found the most horrible thing."

"I know exactly what you found, Madison." His voice sounded ominously low.

He was pushing her now, forcing her back into the office she had just come from.

"What are you doing?" she protested.

"Taking care of another problem," he told her.

"You? *You* did that?" she cried, motioning over her shoulder. She didn't dare turn her back on him.

"I had to. He was going soft on me. Threatening to put an end to our empire. He should have known I would never just *quit*." He practically spat the word.

"What are you talking about? Why would you—"

A cold smile came into his eyes. "Ah, you get it now, don't you? It's all starting to make sense to you."

Her mind raced backwards. Athens. Longview. Both were in East Texas, where Sid claimed he was from. Grandbury. Corpus Christi. Johnson City, and Austin. She had heard the towns and the areas mentioned numerous times lately. They were the places Sid had lived, the places key members of the sweep had lived.

She tried not to gasp. "You're part of it? Part of the sweep?"

He tried not to chuckle. "We didn't call it that back in the beginning. Leon and I were just trying to make a living."

"You were partners?"

McGarvey, aka Sid, shrugged his shoulders. "Partners. Family. Call it what you like."

She felt her mouth fall open. The surprises just kept coming. "You were *kin* to him? And you killed him?"

"You ask a lot of question, you know that?" he snarled. With a flash of anger, he kicked the door shut behind them. "He was my stepfather. We had a good thing going, and then, out of the blue, he says he wants to retire. He wanted to *quit* on me." She heard the pain in his voice, mingled among the anger. "Pops told me I could always depend on him, and then he wants to just up and leave me!"

Madison tried pacifying the man. "I—I'm sure it wasn't like that. I'm sure it had nothing to do with you personally."

"Don't go all psychotherapist on me!" he roared. "I'm the medical professional here, not you!"

Nate was on his way. She needed to stall this madman until he got here, but she also needed answers.

"Yeah, about that. That was quite a career change. When Gray and I knew you, you were an investor."

"Oddly enough," he smirked, "once you've been in prison, people don't seem to trust you with their money."

"Yet they trust you with their body? How did you get licensed?"

"Change of name, change of credentials." His tone was blasé. He waved his hand. "There seemed to be some confusion about the different requirements between states and how the records were transferred."

"Let me guess. New Mexico?"

"That's right. But I found a very lovely young lady—or two—" he grinned lasciviously, "who were more than willing to help me straighten it all out."

Madison's voice dripped with sarcasm. "How nice for you."

McGarvey eyed her with an odd look in his eyes. Was that disappointment? Ridicule? Madison was still trying to decipher the look when he asked, "You aren't going to ask me about the letters?"

"Letters?"

"I know some of them slipped through. I tried to intercept them, but I missed a few." He cocked his head. "You ask so many questions," he said. "Didn't you ask yourself why you would get letters addressed to the firm now, after all these years? Curiosity didn't drive you to open them?"

"I'm confused. *You* sent the letters?"

"You're not listening, Madison. I *received* the letters. They were meant for me. Success is in the details, you know. I've always said good bookkeeping is key to good profits."

As usual, Brash had been right, she thought. The ambiguous descriptions were drug related.

"But... why my address?"

McGarvey spread his hands in a gesture that said, 'why not?'

"I don't have one of my own," he explained. "I had to get them some way, and I knew I would be in The Sisters, working with your new husband. It seemed poetic to send them to my old partner's widow."

Madison recalled the day she left him and Brash alone at the house and the unease she felt in doing so. She thought of the way one letter had disappeared. And the way she hadn't heard the alarm system announce his exit, even when Brash said he was gone for the day. It had happened more than once.

Had he been snooping all that time? Had he been rifling through her mail? Through their mailbox?

While Madison speculated about his devious ways, McGarvey's eyes roamed around the room. She saw him zero in on the desk. She dared to turn her head, trying to see what caught his attention.

Was that a file? A long, narrow, metal file? The kind used to grind hard materials and to smooth rough edges? It could be used to work on restaurant equipment, she reasoned. Would it also work to turn a rock of cocaine into powder? She didn't know much about illicit drugs, but she knew what McGarvey was thinking.

The file would make an excellent dagger.

She was amazed that her voice sounded so calm. "How would you do it?" she challenged him. "How would you explain two bodies in one room, both stabbed to death? Who would believe it?"

"A little staging should do the trick," he said confidently. "Obviously, you took Leon by surprise and stabbed him in the back. He managed to reach the file and defend himself, but it was too late. You both died from your injuries."

"What motive would I have for killing him?"

McGarvey's temper flared again. "That's for the police to decide, not me!"

"You'll—You'll never get away with it," she said. Her voice was no longer so calm. She was in grave danger. This man had killed his stepfather, and he planned to kill her.

"I'm willing to take that chance," McGarvey said with nonchalance. "Seems to me, I've been lucky so far."

The door wasn't that far away. If she could only get around him... She would have to move fast. Faster than him.

He read her thoughts. "Don't try it," he warned.

There was a commotion out in the hallway, and Madison heard her name being called.

"Madison? Madison, where did you go? You just went off and left me!" She heard Miss Wanda complaining from the other side of the door. "Where did you go? Is that you in there?"

The doorknob jiggled, but the door was stuck again. After bumbling and knocking about, the door suddenly burst open, and Wanda stumbled in.

Her bulky form bounced into McGarvey's back and knocked him off balance. As the two of them went down, Madison moved in time to avoid disaster.

McGarvey took the brunt of the fall. His head whacked the edge of the desk before face-planting the floor. As she followed him down, Wanda was fortunate enough to have him for a cushion.

"Miss Wanda! Are you okay?" Madison was already trying to help her up.

"I'm fine. This kind fella here cushioned my fall!" she said with a giggle.

While Madison helped Wanda to her feet, McGarvey groaned. With each jab from the old woman's elbow, he grunted in protest. The floor was beneath him. The woman was on top of him. With pain shooting throughout his body, his moans came out muffled.

Madison almost had her. Just as she pulled Miss Wanda to her feet, she lost her grip on the older woman's arm, and down she went. Again. The hefty woman landed on McGarvey with a thud, knocking the breath out of him.

"Oh, my," she said, taking it all in stride. "Let's try that again." Pushing her hand into McGarvey for a boost, she struggled to sit up.

Nate's deep voice came from the door. "Need a

helping hand?"

"Nate! You're just in time!" Madison cried in relief.

"Here. Let me get her." He sidestepped Madison and had Wanda up in no time, totally unaware of the situation. Brash had simply told him Madison needed his help and to go in without fanfare. "You're sure you're okay?" he asked.

"Oh, I'm fine, just fine," Wanda assured him. She, too, was unaware of the danger she had stumbled into. "It's him I'm worried about." She pointed to the prone man on the floor.

Leaning over McGarvey, Nate asked, "Sir, can I help you up? Are you hurt?"

"You can arrest him, that's what you can do!" Madison said indignantly. "This man is the ringleader of the drug sweep." She pointed in the general direction of Leon's body, still hidden from their view. "And he's a murderer. He killed his partner!"

"Are you sure?" Nate asked sharply.

"See for yourself. His body is right there, on the other side of the desk."

Miss Wanda's eyes lit with excitement. "I've never seen a dead body up close before. Not someone who's been murdered, anyway. Can I look?"

Nate was busy confirming the death. Madison kept an eye on the injured man on the floor. He hadn't tried to get up. He just lay there moaning. With no one stopping her, Miss Wanda followed Nate.

"Oooh, he's dead, all right," she said. "Look at all that blood."

"Get back," Nate warned. He put his hand out to keep her back. "You shouldn't see this. And you could contaminate the scene."

"Oh, pooh. I'm behind you, and he's over there," she protested.

"Miss Wanda, you really should come back over

here," Madison encouraged gently. She was certain the shock would set in soon, and Miss Wanda would be traumatized by what she had witnessed.

Or not. Her reply was all but a whine. "But I can't see from over there."

Nate was on his radio, calling for backup. He didn't need the added worry of a fractious old woman.

Madison said quickly, "I need you here. We have to make sure this one doesn't get away."

"We do?"

"Yes, we do."

Brightening, Miss Wanda turned from one prone body to the other. The last one still posed a danger, which was much more exciting than the one covered in blood.

As she turned her ample hips, Wanda hit one of the many boxes stacked against the desk. The box fell, and an assortment of pills hit the floor, scattering in all directions.

"Watch out!" Madison warned.

It was too late. Wanda had already taken a step forward. The pills rolled beneath her orthopedic shoes, causing her to lose her balance. She aimed for a soft landing, once again falling across McGarvey's body.

This time, she rendered the man unconscious.

"We're good!" she assured Madison with a wide grin. "This murderer's not going anywhere."

21

"Well done, Deputy Stone. I hereby present you with the medal of Exceptional Service in the Line of Duty."

In a formal ceremony at the police station, Brash clipped the gold pin to Nate's uniform. The younger officer leaned down so the chief could reach him while seated.

The ceremony continued with accolades from Brash, Mayor Howell, the county judge, and even a written message of appreciation from the governor. Reporters from area newspapers and the nearest television station were there to document the honors.

Nate was credited for breaking up one of the most notorious and elusive organized crime schemes in the state. New Mexico and Oklahoma had also suffered from their path of destruction.

Almost twenty years ago, Leon Klein and his stepson McGarvey Orr had come up with the concept. After dabbling in the drug trade, Leon was tired of being the underling. The big money was at the top, where it always managed to stay. What paltry little he made was hardly worth the effort.

Using his list of contacts and crooked friends, Leon

set up his own organization. It was a network of men and women who were willing to take a risk. In return for their loyalty, Leon promised to share the wealth.

Still in his mid-twenties, Mac was the one to suggest expanding their reach. Food trucks weren't the rage back then, but it was common enough to see hot dog vendors and simple offerings on city streets. If they could come up with something on wheels, they could expand their business, he claimed.

A plan was formed and set into action. Over the years, they tweaked and polished, until they had the process down to a science. Leon found prime target markets, procured the outlets needed, recruited delivery personnel, and coordinated the drops. Mac called him the wheeler because he set the deals in motion. He claimed the honor of dealer for himself. With his background in finance, he could secure the cash they needed to operate and expand. Even his stint in prison proved useful, putting him in contact with like-minded 'entrepreneurs.'

And it was in prison that he discovered the benefits of being in the medical field. Even physical therapists had access to certain types of drugs. The traveling nurse program gave them access to an even broader audience.

When Nate made his acceptance speech, he said he couldn't have done it without help. He looked directly at Madison when he spoke. For obvious reasons—one of them named Wanda Shanks—he didn't elaborate on who had helped, or in what capacity.

Otis had chosen not to come to the ceremony. He claimed he was covering traffic patrol so the other deputies could share in Nate's special day, but everyone knew the real reason. He had looked no further than the motorcycle gang when confronting the drug problem, and the ceremony was proof of his ineptness. While it was true that the Lucky 13s had benefited from the operation, they weren't directly involved in it as he had insisted. Otis was quietly relieved of his duties as acting chief and had been reassigned. He was now researching the trend of sweeps and other methods preferred by today's criminals.

The loss of his physical therapist had presented a slight setback for Brash, but it was short lived. He worked even harder to recover the strength and full use of his leg. He had finally agreed to a compromise with doctors and, most importantly, with his wife: he could go into the station three days a week, as long as he worked from his chair.

Most days, he managed to keep his word, but only because Vina was worse than Madison. She didn't take any flak from the chief, even if he was her superior.

After Nate's ceremony, Madison invited everyone to the Big House for a reception. Genny provided most of the food. Megan, however, insisted on making Nate's favorite apple praline cake.

"Do you think we'll be having another ceremony before long?" Genny asked her best friend. She nodded to the guest of honor and the way his arm stayed snugly around Megan's waist.

"I don't know." Madison smiled as she watched the young couple. They were clearly in love. "But don't mention that to her father just yet. He's still adjusting to them being in a serious relationship. If you mention marriage, he may have a heart attack!"

Genny laughed and made a locking motion over her lips. "He won't hear it from me."

"And while marriage is certainly nowhere in the picture, I do believe my son will be visiting a little more often in the days to come." Madison discreetly pointed to Blake, who stood between Mindi and Mia Robertson.

Today marked the second time he had been home since meeting the twins just three weeks ago.

No matter the reason, Madison knew she would enjoy having her son home more often. Brash often teased her about being like a mother hen, needing to know her brood was home and safe before she, herself, could relax.

"That would make his ol' auntie glad," Genny said with a smile. The twins referred to her as their aunt, and she called them her niece and nephew. "To be honest, I miss that boy coming in and raiding my refrigerators, whether it's at home or at the restaurant."

"Me, too, but I do enjoy our much lower food bill." Madison laughed.

The smile lingered on her lips as she looked around the house, filled with so many of the faces she loved and adored. There was nothing quite like living in a small town, surrounded by friends and family.

"I'm just glad to see things are getting back to normal around here," she murmured.

It was true. The town was quieter without the motorcycles roaring through. The crime rate was low again. The faces seen around town were familiar. The 'feel' of The Sisters had returned to its easy atmosphere. And the sidewalks remained clean, particularly after Otis was appointed to the new Make The Sisters Shine campaign. Most importantly, Brash was back in his official capacity as the town's peacekeeper. His calm, steadfast leadership made everyone feel safe.

But not everything had stayed the same; there had been some changes, too. A seafood restaurant had taken over the *Oma and Opa's* location. The concept of a food truck park in The Sisters was catching on, but it seemed The Grove at *Myrna's Meadows* was doomed.

The only food trucks left were *Benji's Barbecue* and *Coffee and Cream.*

Surprisingly, a new investor stepped up and breathed new life into the project.

Travis Robertson bought out Myrna Lewis and renamed the RV park *Meadows Lake.* By the time the Christmas holidays came around, he had created The Forest of Light, a drive-through wonderland filled with lighted holiday scenes. The Grove was in full swing by then, with a bandstand that doubled as Santa's special stage, an expanded dance floor, and six food trucks. Mindi and Mia's father had plans to add more vendor spaces for the summer, and there was talk of a possible swimming pool to come.

Even though Granny Bert claimed 'normal' was just a setting on the dryer, Madison knew it was much more than that.

Normal was knowing where her children were, at least in some general sense. Normal was keeping up with her energetic grandmother and her often-crazy-but-always-lovable octogenarian friends. Normal was nosy neighbors and the local grapevine. Normal was noisy family meals at the deCordova Ranch or around Granny Bert's scarred kitchen table. Normal was taking on quirky jobs at *In a Pinch.* Normal was a quiet evening at home with the man she loved.

Life in The Sisters may not have been what some people called 'normal,' but it was the normal she knew and loved.

This normal was what made Madison smile.

Join us for the next anything-but-normal adventure in The Sisters! Debut date to be announced.

If you've enjoyed this installment of the series, please leave a review on Amazon and other sites of your choice. Thank you so much for reading!

I love hearing from readers, so drop in for an e-visit anytime at beckiwillis.ccp@gmail.com.

ABOUT THE AUTHOR

Becki Willis, best known for her popular The Sisters, Texas Mystery Series, Forgotten Boxes, and Keep Your Doors Locked is a best-selling who has won numerous awards. These include two Silver Falchions Awards, a RONE, first place honors for Best Mystery Series, Best Suspense Fiction and Best Audio Book, and many more. She has introduced her imaginary friends to readers around the world.

An avid history buff, Becki likes to poke around in old places and learn about the past. Other addictions include reading, writing, unraveling a good mystery, and coffee. She loves to travel but believes coming home to her family and her Texas ranch is the best part of any trip.

Connect with her at http://www.beckiwillis.com/ or http://www.facebook.com/beckiwillis.ccp.